MW00330485

TRISTAN
AND
Iseult

JD SMITH

TRISKELE BOOKS

Copyright © 2013 JD Smith

The moral rights of the author have been asserted.

All rights reserved. No part of this publication may be
reproduced, distributed, or transmitted in any form or by
any means, including photocopying, recording, or other
electronic or mechanical methods, without the prior written
permission of the publisher, except in the case of brief
quotations embodied in critical reviews and certain other non-
commercial uses permitted by copyright law. For permission
requests, write to the publisher, addressed "Attention:
Permissions Coordinator," at the email address below.

Cover design and formatting www.jdsmith-design.com

Published by Quinn Publications

Printed by Lightning Source UK

All enquiries to editor@quinnpublications.co.uk

First printing, 2013

ISBN 978-0-9576164-0-0

For Marcus, a great reader, who may one day read this.
Rest assured that, although it is a story of love,
it also has swords.

Acknowledgements

My sincere gratitude goes to: Jill and Gilly, for their faith and arm-twisting, together with Liza and Kat of Triskele Books for their editing and support; Perry for his kind words and proofreading; Danny, Lo, JV and all the writers from the Asylum, *Words with JAM* and Facebook for their continuous friendship and encouragement. And Chris, with whom I have not spoken in many years, who once told me that I should write, and so I did.

PART ONE

Promises are a show of faith when doubt shadows men,
a reflection of the person we desire to be,
and a bind to a path we wish to take.
It is the latter likely kept.

CHAPTER 1

Tristan

Rustling emanates from the dense forest, even though the wind has dropped. White mist shrouds us. I tense to stop cold shivers taking hold. The rain is fine, yet a hand through my hair proves it is wetter than the streams in springtime and my footing slides on the muddy grass as we pick our way through undergrowth.

Beside me, Rufus glances at our scouts dotting the countryside. His expression unconcerned as he tries to appear calm.

'I cannot believe the Saxon scum have moved this far west. Who would have thought it, eh, when we were boys?'

Just sixteen. Still a boy, I think. And I am only three years older.

'I wish we were back in Kernow, instead of here in this forsaken place,' he continues. 'I miss the coast and the sea breeze and decent meals.'

I look around. I have little knowledge of how far these lands extend. We are further east than I have ever been, called upon by our neighbour, the King of Dumnonia, to provide a defence, and with luck push the Saxons back. I am told beyond here lies Atrebatia and Lundein, but no Briton has trodden either ground since the invaders claimed them.

'I think this winter is harder than the last,' Rufus says. 'I cannot feel my feet. The bastards better arrive today before we freeze!'

I nod absently. I hear a noise in the distance. Horns, I think, but I cannot be sure. Some say your mind begins to play tricks on you after a while. The cold and the quiet and the waiting; they let thoughts run too free.

Ground mist and fogging breath look the same. Rufus is right: I can no longer feel my toes, despite the layers binding them. Then I know I hear it. The horns … and drum beats.

'Your silence makes me uneasy,' Rufus says.

'Not so loud. The enemy is close.'

Rufus' face is white and his eyes wide in the dawn.

'Are you sure?'

'Listen. Can you hear the drums?'

I snap my head from one side to the other, trying to determine their location. Rufus falls silent and listens, too. I see other scouts smelling the air, sensing the Saxons drawing close.

'I hear it,' he says.

'They are cowards,' I whisper. 'They come from the woods so they can hit and retreat. A stream to our left. Uneven ground to the right. We cannot flank them here.'

As I speak, the forest shimmers and dark figures emerge.

'Gods, you are right. Why are you not giving the orders, eh? Under the Dumnonian's command, we might as well be led by a woman.'

I know how he feels. Each man is as safe as the skill of the warriors beside him and that of the men leading him. Here we are brothers and must trust one another. But trust the Dumnonians? They let the invaders cross their borders and now they need our help. What trust does that deserve?

'Stop worrying,' I say. 'This is Dumnonian territory. We will be home again soon enough.'

'I wish I had your belief,' he says.

The men lining the edge of the forest grow clearer in the still air.

Rufus tugs on my arm.

'We must go back and report their progress.'

The enemy's chanting grows louder. They want our army to hear them. They want to put fear in our hearts and make the hands that hold our swords tremble.

I put my own hands beneath my arms to warm them ready for the moment when I'll need to grip my sword. I have unsheathed it many times this day already to ensure it does not stick in its scabbard. It is a Roman blade; better forged than all the iron in Briton.

'Let's move before they see us,' I say, as signals relay back and forth between the distant scouts, barely visible in the mist.

We slide our way back to our mounts.

'We have been lucky,' Rufus says. 'We encountered the Saxon three times this winter. Three times we have walked away with our lives. Do you think we can do it again?'

He is grinning like a confident fool. I know that look. Hesitation and a question linger behind the smile.

'How long will the gods' favour last? With luck a few more battles at least.'

His expression falters.

'Listen to me, Rufus. Listen carefully.' He slips and I grip his arm to steady him. 'Are we not better fighters than the Dumnonians?'

He nods.

I say: 'Then if we fall, we fall last and we fall hard. That is all you need to know. In the meantime, enjoy yourself.'

I am unsure I believe my own words. I have caused my cousin injuries with a wooden sword more times than I have picked him from the ground after a fall or consoled all the girls whose hearts he has broken. I do not wish to lie to him. I could never twist truths as other men do. But he needs me, does little Rufus. He needs me to be strong for him. How long can a man stand in battle before the odds turn against him? Luck will see us right for a while. Then it will fade, just as everything in this accursed world.

We reach the horses. Mine snorts in irritation at having to

postpone grazing as I heave myself up into the saddle and drag on the reins to pull the beast round.

'Hurry, Rufus.'

I do not like being so close to the enemy. Their ways are strange. They rub their skin with stinking fat and howl like dogs. I hear their wails and chants echoing across the muddy scrubland. They will send their own scouts ahead and I do not want them to close the distance between us.

Rufus fumbles his foot into a stirrup. Impatience grips me until he finally hauls himself up and we are away, the horses' footing careful on the sodden ground.

Our warriors fall out either side of an old Roman road. Many lift skins of mead to their lips to fire courage, suspecting this will be the day to fight, or else they heat their blood to stave off the damp that tickles their joints. Faces are grey and dirty and tired as they look at us expectantly. Servants take our mounts and Rufus and I pick our way through the mass of men without a word to anyone. They know, I am sure, what news we deliver. But they will wait; King Geraint must hear it first.

The Dumnonian king stands with his councillors. They listen to another scout and the king's head moves up and down as the man gives his report, telling him the invaders do not appear to be in the north lands at present. When the scout has finished, the king flicks a hand and the scout is ushered away. Geraint beckons Rufus and me forward.

'What news, Rufus ap Mark?'

He stares at my cousin in earnest. His eyes are too close together, and his face is gaunt with worry. I am told he no longer eats, for a growth inside his belly leaves little room for food.

My cousin glances to me, but Geraint does not address me, and Rufus needs to prove himself.

'Their army has moved, my Lord. They are waiting for us on the edge of the forest, half a mile east.' Rufus pauses. 'There is a stream on one side and rocky ground on the other. If we face them there, we cannot flank them.'

He speaks with confidence and I smile inwardly at his remembering my words.

King Geraint glances at the ground and then around at the men sharpening their blades, cleaning their armour, cooking breakfast over embers still glowing from the night before.

'Damn them!' the king mutters. 'Damn the pagans to a Christian hell, every last one of them.'

I flinch at his use of *pagan* when so many men of Briton still worship the old gods, but I say nothing.

'We must face them today,' another man growls. A scar carves his beard in two and he has only three teeth in a savage mouth. 'They are too close to our settlements already. We cannot afford to yield any more of Dumnonia.'

I check my blade again. Habit, I know, but I need to be ready. The day wears on. The sun has not yet broken through. The chill of morning still bites.

'Is there a way around the forest?' I ask.

'We should not split our force,' the scarred man grunts.

'Who says to split it?' I reply. 'Sparing a few men to suggest we are located here, I say we move all our warriors to their rear. Cut them off from their own people and make a dent that will see them retreat until summer at least.'

Everyone looks to me. I shrug and turn away, as if my words were merely a suggestion of no importance.

'What is your name?' the king demands.

'Tristan.'

'Your father?'

'I have no father.' The words are so familiar I do not think of their meaning as I speak them.

Geraint's look hardens as he waits.

'My uncle, King Mark, speaks for me.'

'Are you trying to amuse me, Tristan ap Mark?' the king says, his tired eyes irritable, the lines of his forehead deeper. 'To move our men and leave the Saxon a clear path into the heart of my kingdom?'

'No, my Lord.'

The scarred man's breath plumes as he stands beside Geraint. Sores on his cheeks weep down his face and into his beard.

I glance to Rufus in reassurance, for I know he is nervous. 'Your father would agree,' I say to him, 'if he were here.'

'Mark is not here,' the King of Dumnonia replies lightly, flicking a hand to the warriors surrounding us. 'He did not think our cause worthy of his personal attention. He did not come himself.'

Geraint's words might be light, but his fur-covered shoulders are huge and the sword at his waist well used. I do not wish to antagonise him.

'He sent his son,' I reply, gesturing to Rufus, 'and me, whilst he faces the Irish threat to our own lands. He can give you no more.'

Geraint pulls a hand through his beard without reply.

Rufus was right: I wish the Kernish were in command.

That Mark were here.

Chapter 2

Iseult

I lie on the gritty shore. My eyes are closed and my hair is full of sand. The wind drags spray that dries on my lips. I taste it: salty, abrasive, clean. Gulls cry overhead. I am cold and the ground and the air and my skirts are all damp. I shiver. Close my eyes tighter. Stop them watering. Prevent the tears trailing more salt down my cheeks.

In the distance, my mother calls. Her voice carries on the wind, my name distorted. Dawn has come quickly. I have been here since the early hours. She worries about me, or perhaps she feels guilt.

I do not call back; she will find me in time. I think of celebrations that will commence when our men are home, the food and the drink and the dancing. The music. I will play the harp as I always do. We will toss up in the air the coins our warriors have taken, and listen as they clink and clatter and ring on the floors of our feasting halls. We will sleep when our bellies are full and our eyes tired, and the day after we will be merry once more.

My mother approaches. She has long pale hair like my own, and it whips across her face and her skirts cling to her legs as she strides along the shore towards where I lie. Even from this distance, I can sense her irritation. As she grows nearer, I see her furrowed brow and hard mouth.

'Everyone has been looking for you. I thought you'd been swept off by the tide. Lost in some foreign land,' she says, drawing close.

I get to my feet and brush sand and grit from my clothes. Stagger a little. I have been lying on the ground too long and my limbs are drained of life and my head light.

'Where have you been?' she demands.

Looking about me, I say: 'Here. I have been here all the time.'

'The whole night?'

I do not answer. There is no point. She does not want excuses; she wants to be angry. So I let her.

'Speak to me …'

'I watched the sun break the night.'

'You go nowhere alone,' she says. 'You take your maid and one of our warriors with you everywhere. I cannot have you wandering the shores alone in the dark, or at any other time.'

'Of course, Mother.'

'Our lord will not stand for your independent ways, your selfishness and your disobedience,' she says.

I knew that was the reason for her impatience. She is concerned for our lord's temperament above all else.

I must look weary at her words, for she continues: 'Our position is not secure. Not until he is king and you have his heir in your belly. Only then will we maintain our position within the tribe.'

I flinch at her words. When our lord returns home this time, I am to be his wife. I will do what I am requested to do. Submit to the man who leads our people. Be honoured I am chosen above all others to sit beside our strongest warrior.

Morholt.

'Our uncles ensure our safety,' I reply.

'Do not be stupid, child.' Her voice pierces the wind as shrill as the gulls. 'They rule in the north. Morholt has an understanding with them only because they do not have enough men to command these southern lands, and neither are they interested. Be assured, Morholt's power in these parts increases with each passage to Briton. He has them squirming on what is left of their pitiful island.'

We walk in silence a while. I think of Morholt. How he takes the girls of our tribes to his bed. I hear them, sometimes, screaming and crying and whimpering. I cannot imagine what he does to them; I dare not imagine. But in the mornings their faces are bruised and swollen, skin broken, bodies bloodied. They will not talk of it. They are afraid, just as I am afraid.

My safety was assured when my father ruled over these lands. My mother is still Queen in name, but no longer possesses any power; not until the union she seeks is complete. I am a queen's daughter. So he has been savouring the moment when he can take me — a woman of the blood — for his own, and secure not only his strength over men, but a rightful heir.

'Father always said we could call upon our uncles if we needed to.'

'Your father is dead.'

I want to cry for the unfeeling manner in which she refers to him. She cared for him, but the anxiety caused by his passing has taken its toll and she is no longer the woman she once was. I hear whispers Morholt killed my father, and she has heard them too. They may be true, for he is a man to be feared above all other men; a man who raids foreign countries to swell our lands with gold; who covers his warriors' shields in the blood of those who stand against him.

As a girl I sat with my father's men, cross-legged in wheat fields, and painted our shields red with sheep-blood. My father said it was to frighten our enemies, but Morholt says they know it is not human. So he hangs those he captures in raids; hangs them in the barn and drives blades into their necks and lets their blood drain into buckets. He lines the bodies on our shore to face the kingdoms beyond the sea. Then he uses the blood to paint our men's shields, drying dark and brown.

Our lord is a man without mercy, whose purpose is simply to amuse himself. He does not acknowledge any god, nor does he fear them as others do. Wary, yes, but never frightened of the wrath that might bring down upon us. He laughs in the face of the higher rulers, the ones even kings fear. And he no longer allows us to pray.

But I do. I pray each morning and each night. I pray on my knees before an altar in a cave on the shore where my father once used to give sacrifice. I pray because I am frightened of what is to come …

We walk homewards along the shore in silence. I think of praying again, hoping that Morholt will not return to us.

He will take me as his wife, terrify our people, gain in power until none can stand against him. And I will watch and do nothing, for there is nothing to be done.

My name and my blood will make him a king of Ireland.

CHAPTER 3

Tristan

The Saxon wait, just as we Kernish and Dumnonians wait. I shift from one foot to the other, trying to restore the flow of blood. My shield feels too tight on my arm. The mist of early morning has begun to clear and the watery sun casts a yellow glow. Four hundred yards ahead, arrayed in a deep line, the enemy howl a war cry and scream in their foreign tongue.

Our own line stands calm. We could match their shouts, indeed some murmur restlessly. I prefer our quiet. It puts a greater fear in a man. I feel that fear, but steel in my hand gives me a comfort I cannot describe, its weight heavy and hard edge reliable.

To my left, Rufus scratches his chest.

'Will you desist,' I say.

'Being in Dumnonia makes me itch.'

'You cannot hold a sword and a shield whilst you are seeing to itches, you whelp!'

He stops and picks up his sword from the muddy grass. Dries the hilt on his tunic.

'That will be the last time I scratch your back,' he says.

'I have a sword. I will scratch it with that.'

'Ha! Only if you wish to shave the hairs from it.'

Our banter tails as King Geraint approaches. More furs bulk his figure and I feel lean beside him. A slight limp hinders his stride and uncertainty weighs down rounded shoulders. The man with the scar does not accompany him, instead he stands at the fore of the group waiting for the slaughter to commence.

The king ushers us to him with a gloved hand.

'Rufus, Tristan, come,' he says, our names emphasised with firmness.

We follow. Back beyond the line barely two men deep that stretches the narrow pass; the only force between the Saxon and Dumnonia. Dumnonia and Kernow.

Five hundred paces and we sink into a larger group of warriors. Geraint drops the furs from his shoulders. Armour stretches across a rounded belly and warrior bands grip thick arms. They must be old bands, for he has won little of late. A sword is passed to him. He fastens the belt tight and accepts his shield.

'Are we ready?'

A rumble of agreement and a low rattle of swords against shields.

I scan the solemn faces. Dumnonians. Eyes half closed with fatigue, limbs shaking with cold, muscles wasted from a raided harvest. Spirits waning. I know they are unsure we can prevail. Mark would have fed them before any other in the kingdom — our protectors — bolstered their morale to make a confident band of warriors. Mark would do many things differently, but Geraint lets his lords take first tithe, and there is little provision in the borderlands to swell the food we are given.

Our small force moves south, leaving the two thin lines behind. Mud drags at my feet with every step. Some chatter nervously, but the older, seasoned warriors hiss for silence. Leather creaks in time with our pace. My fingers are numb. I tense my grip on both sword and shield, release and tense again, trying to bring life back.

Geraint has acknowledged my suggestion. He knows another head-on battle would see an end to Dumnonia, to more of Briton. His warriors are better trained; disciplined in the Roman way and yet our numbers diminish with each year as the Saxon become stronger. The position of our people weakens as Geraint calls on all the lords.

I thought the king would stay with our feint; his huge, bear-like figure with his army, further persuading the Saxon our force remains to their fore.

Instead he leads us.

We reach a beck. Small, but too wide to jump. I clamber down into the freezing water, gasp as I slither a couple of feet across, and hoist myself up at the other side. I turn to see Rufus' face, tense against the cold. He thrusts his sword and shield at my feet and tries to pull himself out. His hands are too cold to grip properly and he slips back into the water. I grab his arm and haul him up.

All along the beck others are doing the same: helping their brothers across and onto the slick earth, weed and debris.

Rufus' jaw quivers with the cold.

'How far?'

We are making a loop out before circling back on the Saxon. I doubt they will hear us now, but he whispers anyway. He looks a little startled, as he did when we faced a small force in the north two months ago. He almost got himself killed, then. He broke our wall and for that many warriors are wary of butting their shield next to his. You protect the man next to you with your shield, and the man on your other side protects you. Break and brothers are exposed. You let them down.

I persuade myself it was not cowardice. He is young. He needs to learn, that is all; learn that you do not break for anything or anyone. You hold. Hold fast.

Afterwards, I beat him as his father would have done, for being a simpleton, because he is more like my brother than my cousin.

'Not long now. We are over half way,' I say.

He breathes heavily beside me as we trudge on, more from a rush of anticipation than any exertion, I suspect. My own breathing is slow and controlled.

'Do you think they know?' he asks.

'That we will strike their arse whilst they shout insults at a few old warriors waving their swords?'

Rufus smiles weakly as we hurry on. 'What if they do?'

'Doubtful,' I say. 'They are Saxon. They will be drunk.'

CHAPTER 4

Iseult

Acha is watching me. We are in my bedchamber and she combs my hair. She is twice my age, with a face that is beginning to crease when she smiles and a wariness that tells me she is not happy with the role my mother has given her: to watch over me, I suspect. Because I like to walk along the beach as the light begins to emerge, signalling a new day.

A ship has been spotted on the horizon. Our people are sure it is our warriors returning from Briton. When they left they said they would return to us in five days, and today is the sixth day. Lord Morholt leads them, and I pray and pray he does not come back; that the men of Kernow have taken his life and unknowingly saved me from an unwanted union.

'What I would give for hair as fair as yours, Iseult,' Acha says, as she teases the comb through tangles.

I feel myself grow hot.

'Because you comb and dress it,' I reply. 'Without you it would be tangled with seaweed.'

She laughs.

'And full of sand, too.'

I know she is avoiding talk of our men's return, even though they are close. She knows better than any that I fear becoming Morholt's bride and do not wish to talk of it. His face lurks in my mind and turns my stomach like the morning after a night of mead.

She continues combing in silence for some time. Then finally she says: 'Please, do not wander any more. You have me in trouble enough with your mother, without disappearing every other night.'

'Oh, Acha, I am sorry. I never thought ...'

'It is all right. Just promise me you will not keep doing it. My nerves play me terribly!'

I turn to face Acha and see her worried expression; caught between my mother and me. We are close, and my mother knows it.

'I am sorry,' I say again.

'Do not be daft, child.' She pulls a smile onto her face and kisses the top of my head fondly. 'Come now,' she turns me back so she can finish my hair, 'we must be ready for...'

Her words go unfinished. Awkwardness follows in which neither of us speaks. She ties ribbons into my hair and weaves them around the strands, intertwining and curling until hair frames my face with flecks of silver and gold and trails over my shoulders.

'We must be ready for Morholt's return,' I say eventually, and my own sadness is loud in my ears.

'We must.'

Tears well and I cannot keep them back. They spill down my cheeks and I brush them away and try to hide my face.

'Och, come now. Everything will be all right. You'll see.'

Acha pulls my hands from my face and dries it with her skirts.

'You are young, and this world is a very old place. In time you will know worse than lying with a man you would rather not. Get with child quickly and he'll not visit you again. I promise.'

I am unsure I believe Acha. She is more of a mother than my own. I care for her dearly. But for our closeness I know she would lie to comfort me.

'When I become his wife, you will stay with me? Do not leave me alone.'

It is the first time I have shown how afraid I really am. My mother is a woman who admits nothing. I see her hurt, and her discomfort, and her tiredness, and that she misses my father, but she will never say it or look to be consoled. So now I am weak because of the words I dare to utter.

'Bless you,' Acha says, as if I am but a silly child with no reason to worry. 'Of course I'll stay with you. I've not left you these many years now, have I? Why would I leave now?'

I do not know why I asked. She knows, as I do, that she may not have a say. Morholt could send her away with nothing to be done, and I would be alone with only my mother, who lets the days slide by with little joy.

Acha and I grip one another in a tight embrace, which is more comfort than any words. Behind me, I hear footsteps. A moment later my mother's voice:

'We must head to the shore. Our ships have landed.'

I pull away from Acha, careful not to turn and let my mother see my face.

'I am coming.'

I sense her pause. Then in words that convey no warmth she says: 'For all our sakes, Iseult, do not displease our lord.'

CHAPTER 5

Tristan

Our group makes a path through the forest to the rear of the Saxon force. Dark, dense, sweet with rotting foliage: punctuated by the smell of shit where the lazy bastards have not the mind to dig a hole. Dying fires litter the ground where they ate the night before and carcasses of Dumnonian livestock scatter the moss. I hear the low rumble of warriors not far away; shouting and drumming spears on shields. Cursing.

A Dumnonian boy, the same age as Rufus – not lean but scrawny – pauses to pull a lump of still fresh meat from the bones of a doe. He shoves it into his mouth and chews frantically. An older warrior claps a hand over the boy's mouth, punches his head with the butt of his sword and shoves him onward.

My own stomach grumbles, empty and aching. But I run on, swift and sure of my footing. Over a hundred warriors and we make barely a sound save for the twigs beneath our feet complaining of passage. The king is ahead; eyes alert, darting; sword, as mine, held ready.

I spot the back of Saxon warriors a few hundred yards away; furs padding huge figures, helmets encasing their heads. The smell of mead heavy on the air.

Our group begins to slow.

A gesture from Geraint brings us level. Trees shadow us. Our attack delayed with every moment concealed. I have broken a light sweat and there is no breeze to cool me. I rub the side of my face on my shoulder and draw a few long breaths.

Rufus stares ahead. He holds his sword in front of him. It wavers slightly, and I notice sweat breaks on his brow also.

'They are greater in number than last time,' he says.

I judge them for myself. Their number is not as large as he thinks.

'Keep your head, Rufus,' I say in a whisper. 'It is just like last time and the time before. We go in, we attack. Think only about the man coming at you. And kill him.'

Rufus gives a small nod. He is wearing his father's old armour. I recall when Mark gave it to him. He wanted his son to have the best, to be protected against the enemies we would meet in Dumnonia. Rufus is proud of his father, of his country, of the people that will one day be his. He polishes the scales for hours at a time, because he wants his father to be proud of him in return. To see what a warrior he could become.

Scales rust fast in the damp air.

Men of Kernow catch my eye and press their shield arms to their chests. I gesture back and nod. All our men do the same. Feuds matter not in these moments; we put aside any grudges and become brothers. We will fight the enemy as one. Dumnonians look to each other, raise a sword in salute, but there is less conviction in those men. Their bond is not as ours. Not as close. Too long have they found a need to protect themselves and their families. And for all the requirement and desire to have us here, these proud warriors believe they can manage alone.

Waiting.

I hate the waiting. I can hear my own breathing, steady and coarse. I hear everything: men sniffing back dripping noses, creaking leather, scrapes of iron, whispered orders ... pleas to the gods. Loud; so loud. I am surprised the enemy does not notice our presence.

I almost fall forward in anticipation of the command to charge. It does not come. Not yet.

I want to be in a shield wall, but it will not be possible this time. We need to attack quickly, surprise them. Halt to form a wall and we lose that.

I think again on Rufus' words, wishing Mark were here, in command. It is hard, putting trust in a lord who is not your own. Mark trusted me to come here with Rufus and ensure our men were led by the Dumnonians wisely. Difficult, when you are following their lead.

My thoughts are taking over now. Gods, I wish Geraint would call the …

'Briton!'

The king's roar pierces the rumble of Saxon chants. Geraint begins to run, and I run too, matching his charge. Howling the name of our country, our lands; the lands the Saxon are trying to take from us.

I step clumsily at first. I find my footing. Legs steady and I close the gap. Drag my heavy blade across a man's throat. Shock shows on his face and in his eyes. His head begins to roll back. Blood sprays my face.

I step past him before his knees hit the ground. Drive my Roman blade at the next in line. The iron glances on deep furs and the bastard bares his teeth and screams at me as he lifts his own blade. I am already pulling my sword round and up, deep into his groin. An axe comes towards me. I let my shield take the blow, bludgeon the man with my sword. Hit again and again. Wary of my back. Knowing the whole Saxon force has turned to engage us.

The thud of weaponry on shields all along the enemy line — the war cry as we engage — is deafening. My voice lost in the rage. The Saxons did not know we were coming. I see it their faces; shock in wide eyes. Their movement is unsure, weapons awkward in their hands. But they are also angry. They are brutes. Huge men bringing down their blades with force, not skill. I smell them. Their sweat and dirt and foreign stench. Their madness.

I strike over and over. Moving lithely. Never still. And I think of nothing and no one.

Bloodlust has taken hold and my duty is to kill; simply kill every last stinking Saxon that would take our lands for their own.

CHAPTER 6

Iseult

I am standing in the same place I lay this morning, where my mother found me. The wind is stronger and the sea's spray cold on my cheeks and nose and neck. A crescent moon is clear in the sky, even though it is day, and spittle-flecked waves scurry towards me, then retreat.

Hundreds of warriors, old men, women and children, snake the shoreline. They talk and eat. Boys wrestle on the shingle and in the grass, sprint across the sand and leave footprints in their wake. My mother speaks with the other women of our tribe; those wed to the men with power: council members, warlords, elders. She is desperate to hold her place amongst our people. When at my father's side, they would gather around *her*, praise her, ask her advice. Now she is one of the gatherers. Sometimes I think she would like to be with a man again. But she is too old to bear more children. Acha whispered to me once that my mother offered herself to Morholt, and that he refused her in preference for me, still a woman of the blood, yet young enough to provide an heir.

I look back out to sea, my eyes pinched against the sun. A little way off is the outline of our ship, riding the waves back from Briton. Carrying gold.

Acha pulls her shawl about her.

'I've seen too many years to stand in the cold,' she says. 'Gods speed them so I can return to the fireside.'

The hairs on my arms stand proud, the skin tight. I shiver and link her arm.

'You are not so old, but I agree that the fireside be preferable this night.'

Small boats are carried to the shore on lapping waves, bobbing up and down. Filled with our warriors. I try to see if Morholt is amongst them, but I cannot make him out. Men jump from a boat and it grinds on the shore and water tugs their legs; tries to pull them back.

The warriors ascend the incline to where we stand. Morholt, I see now, is at the head of them, his face hard. Matted hair is clipped back and his beard heavy with plundered jewels. A shudder runs through me.

My mother and a group of our men walk to meet them.

'You return to us well, my Lord?' I hear my mother say. Her voice is courteous. She wants his attention, to ensure we stay favoured even though her position will guarantee it.

'Aye,' he replies, and brushes past her to talk in low tones with his men.

Once his back is turned, she catches my eye. There is loathing, as if it is my fault he does not honour her with gifts. And I see embarrassment and shame in the slight downturn of her head and the flush in her high cheeks.

I am simply thankful he has taken no heed of my presence.

I expect the men to unload the tribute taken from Briton. Instead Morholt heads to our hall and our people follow, whispering. I think we are all nervous of him, of his mood and his temper and what has happened in Briton.

In our hall the fires have been built and stoked and tended. The heat hits my face as I enter; sore on wind-burnt cheeks. Then the sting subsides and I appreciate the warmth our feasting place offers, thankful that Acha's old bones will ease their objections.

Acha and I sit at the top table in the same place we always sit. Only now the largest of chairs is not empty. Morholt fills it and his warriors — his followers — the seats beside him. I am careful not to look into his eyes. If I do not meet them, it is as though I am hidden from him and he will not recall my existence.

We eat. Every morsel taking an age to chew and swallow as our people mutter and gesture and cast guarded looks to our leader. Morholt eats and drinks relentlessly. His cheeks bulge as he chews and mead mixes with every mouthful. The man beside him tries to talk with him, but Morholt does not reply and his face grows ever more discoloured and dangerous.

Finally he stands before our people. His eyes rove the room, looking for something … someone.

'Iseult.'

Slowly, uncertainly, I lift my head and look across to our lord, the man who will become our king; who is already our king in all but name. Time looks unkindly upon his face and his head is unsteady with drink. His eyes are fixed on me.

'My Lord,' I say. At least I think I say it, for I do not hear my own words.

'Play, Iseult.'

'Play?'

'The harp, Iseult,' he says, his voice monotone and daunting. 'Play the harp. I like to hear it. I like to hear you of all our fair women playing it. You ease my thoughts.'

Beneath the table Acha grips my leg in concern before I push back my chair and stand. A few places to my right, my mother glares in irritation as if I do not move fast enough.

'My Lord,' I say. 'What do you wish me to play?'

But Morholt has sat down once more and is now talking with his men, his mood apparently lifted by the prospect of music, and my voice is lost in the mist of chatter.

I play and our people become steadily drunk and Morholt's mood appears ever lighter. Briton is forgotten, his displeasure soaked in drink and hidden behind merriment. I relax, the music drifts from my fingertips and distracts my mind.

As the fires die and the night grows cold, our people wander to their rooms or sleep where they lie. Morholt sits slumped over the table. Cups are scattered all about. Dogs find the courage to steal from the table as their masters sleep. My mother has long since retired and I am thankful she has, for her mood has not lightened as our lord's has.

Acha approaches me as I continue to play.

'It is time to sleep, child,' she says.

Her voice is loud in the quiet hall and I worry it will wake Morholt. I am equally afraid to cease plucking the strings for the silence that might also cause him to stir.

'Iseult,' she says, taking my arm.

We leave the hall and I follow her to our rooms. She pulls off my dress and helps me into a light shift; I do the same for her. Then we cuddle together in the bed for warmth.

I feel safe for the moment. For tonight.

CHAPTER 7

Tristan

'The day for this life has past!'

The Saxon cannot understand Geraint's roar, just as we cannot understand their howling tongue. I am tired and my limbs are both fire and death. I move slowly, careful with my energy. Striking to kill as I finish the last of this battle. Gods give me the strength to continue, for the fear no longer drives me forward.

I stumble upon the bodies of the fallen: Saxon, Dumnonian, Kernish …

They are everywhere and part of me wants to look for the faces of the brothers that we will have lost. Concentrate. It will keep me alive.

The war cry of my people leaves my lips. I almost lose the grip on my sword as I let the weight of it crash into another bastard enemy. I hear the groans of the dying and smell the blood of a hundred men in the air. A haze of red floats before my eyes. Air burns my throat and lungs and my head feels light.

To my right Geraint hammers blows upon the enemy. A frenzy of cuts and slashes. I look for the next man to meet my blade. I see few Saxon. Relief soaks me as I realise we are winning and the last of the Saxon are trying to turn from us into the two lines left at their fore, or falling to the ground.

Muttering a prayer of thanks to the gods, I stumble across to where Rufus squats beside a tree, retching. We have not eaten so nothing comes up. He is pale and as I take his arm to help him to his feet he is shaking so hard I grip him tight to steady him. All about us the remains of the Dumnonian warband howl and shriek their victory. But it is no triumph. I see our men scattered on the ground, slain, their families' prospects and safety draining away like the blood that seeps into this cold, wet earth.

'Rufus. Look sharp. You are being watched.'

Rufus wipes his mouth on his arm. I take his sword from him and stoop down, tear grass. Wipe the blade clean. Rufus has killed again, we all have: lives taken so that one day we may live in some ideal of peace that will likely never be known.

The sword clean, I hand it back to Rufus and he sheaths it.

'How many of our own are lost?' he asks.

'The Dumnonian loss is more than ours. And the enemy loss is higher still.'

Not one Saxon remains standing. Some of them writhe on the ground, but our warriors have not the compassion to end their misery.

'Get moving,' I hear one commander call, referring to the men looting the dead.

We would not want to be here when a larger Saxon force arrives. I wish everyone would hurry. I am tired, weak, thirsty, and I want nothing more than to return to camp and sleep.

'Come on,' I say to Rufus, but he is examining a gash on his thigh.

I stoop down and pull his hand away. The wound is crying red streaks down his leg.

'A scratch,' I say. 'We will clean it when we are back.'

We walk back to the camp without uttering a word. Gaps linger in our lines as if we save spaces for the brothers we have lost. I avoid my fellows' eyes; sure that every man is grateful that we make our way back to camp instead of waiting for the boatman to take us to the Otherworld.

Rufus limps from the cut to his leg. He keeps a brave face and makes no complaint, no sound of any kind.

We arrive back and I peel off my armour. Dried blood cracks. The stench of sweat and leather is pungent. I beckon Rufus down to the stream where we wade into the cold water. I see there are grazes on my arms and legs and my face is stinging, too.

'I will be as scarred as your father by this time next year,' I say to Rufus.

Rufus smiles but says nothing. It is the sort of smile that holds no joy.

Later we eat. Quickly. Wanting only to see our beds and savour the knowledge of being in battle and surviving.

'We beat them,' Rufus says, as we lay side by side that night.

Other men murmur in their sleep, betraying their fears of battle when in the day they know nothing of weakness. I stare into the darkness and whistle a long sigh. We survived once more but how much longer will it last? Another fight, two perhaps?

'We will crush them until not a single Saxon remains on this island,' I say.

How empty those words are. Every time we face these bastards the odds become lower. The Saxon increase in number as their ships land on the east coast, yet our numbers diminish with every battle, the only men left either infants or the crippled.

'We must write to my father in the morning,' he says. 'Tell him of our progress.'

I lean on my arm to face him. His immediate shock of battle has gone, replaced with excitement at yet another victory. He is riding on the alternate waves of fear and elation.

'You write to him, Rufus. Tell him from me that he has every reason to be proud of his son.'

Rufus nods. 'When I am king, I will rule as well as my father.'

I smile at the earnestness in his voice. So many men are corrupted by power. Our cousin, Oswyn, is one such man. But

Rufus is not.

'Mark is a great man and a better king, Rufus. Do him justice and you will know respect.'

We lie in silence a while. I hear other men snoring or talking. Some men cannot sleep after battle, the haunting of the dead keeping them awake. I am one such man.

'What I would give for a woman,' Rufus says. 'A beautiful woman to take my mind off Saxon scum.'

'Do not think about women whilst sleeping next to me.'

'I shall face the other way.' Rufus grins.

'Still not sure I am happy with that arrangement. You talk in your sleep.'

'I do not!'

'Yes you do. I know the name of every woman you ever rutted!'

'Even I do not know that!'

Rufus soon drifts into slumber. I lie awake for a while listening to his shallow breathing and worry about what will come. Rufus may one day become a leader of men, but he has never shown that strength of character yet. He shies away from confrontation, lets other men dictate what is right and make decisions for him; looks to others for guidance. But little Rufus is his father's son, I am sure. He can be the leader we need when his father passes. And with luck that will be a long time from now.

I wake. Pull the blanket up around my shoulders to stave the chill of night. It is still dark and I hear owls. Beside me, Rufus groans and I realise it was he that woke me.

'Rufus!'

I nudge him.

He moans.

'Rufus, the camp stirs.'

He looks as I feel. Tired and wasted. Eyes thin slits above blue rings. Bruising on his cheeks, yellow and fresh. I feel the draw of brotherhood.

'I could sleep all day and another night,' he says.

'There will be time for that. Our army stirs and we need to move. The Saxon will send a force twice as large when they discover what we have done. They are like the tide.'

'We will never go home, will we?' He rubs his face as though washing.

'Of course we will go home. Kernow is but two days away.'

'No, Tristan. That was not what I meant.'

'Then what?'

'The Saxon, they will always come, and we will never escape them. We will never be enough to win. A frontier will always exist and warriors will forever need to defend it.'

His words strike me. I pause a moment. Partly because they are true, and partly because I have never heard him speak with such clarity. He is right. We will never be free of threat. Not unless we scourge Briton of every last Saxon.

It seems impossible.

'Concentrate on the little fight,' I say, 'and the battle will take care of itself.'

I am right that the enemy would come.

We collect our dead the following morning. The scouts have returned, telling us the Saxon are a couple of hours east; a force larger than we have seen before. This time we will not survive if we face them.

But this time Rufus and I will not have to.

CHAPTER 8

Iseult

I wake in a dark room and the night is so cold my breath is a cloud of white. Acha argues in the doorway. I slide from the bed and cross to her to find one of Morholt's men with his booted foot forcing the door open.

'What is it, Acha?'

'Nothing, child. Go back to your bed.'

'She is to come with me,' the man says. Acha is tall, but he is taller still, stooping to see under the lintel. Hair and beard surround his head and face so that all I can see are fractious eyes.

'No.' Acha blocks the doorway and I am sheltered behind her.

The man reaches past Acha, locks his grip on my arm and pulls me down the hallway with him. My heart thuds. I do not know where he is taking me. Behind me, Acha runs to keep up; sobs for him to stop.

We come to a halt outside a door. The man brushes Acha away.

'Go back to your room,' he barks.

'I will stay here,' Acha protests.

Tears begin to run down her cheeks. I feel nothing. I do not know what is happening. I am a rabbit in danger: startled.

Another man — one of Morholt's favoured warriors —

approaches and drags Acha away. Now there is just me and the man who came for me.

He taps on the door and he does not wait for a response, but enters.

'The Queen's daughter, my Lord.'

I am ushered into the room and the door closes behind me and my lord and I are alone.

Morholt.

He paces. Lumbering steps across the wooden floors. He reaches for a cup and sloshes mead on the floor and I know the evening's drink has yet to fade.

He walks across to me.

'You play the harp well.' He speaks as though the matter irrelevant, a mere courtesy he deigns to display.

I do not move. I let his breath roll over my face, clinging to my skin, as he says: 'We are to be husband and wife, Iseult.'

My stomach twists and knots and my legs are weak beneath me. I am afraid, of him and what will happen in this room this night.

'As you desire, my Lord.'

'*Desire?*' He says the word as though it offends him, the very idea of desire ridiculous. 'I do not *desire* you. You arouse no desire in me. You are the daughter of my predecessor — a man who would let the northern kings govern him as he sat on a throne gifted only by his brothers' will and nothing more. He could have been their dog and had more freedom to rule as he wished. I need strong sons, sons combining my blood with the blood of your family, that is all.' He slurs the mention of my father with detestation. He, too, desired only power, and I think how strangely alike their desires are.

'I see the way you look at me, Iseult. You loathe me because you fear me, but it makes no difference. We will be a powerful match, your family ruling the north of Ireland and I with equal strength the south. We will never face invasion as the Britons do. They are so weak they are almost overrun with vermin.'

'Of course, my Lord.'

Anger flares in his eyes at my continued compliance. I aim to please him, so that he might treat me with kindness, perhaps even respect, but I appear to antagonise him even more.

'The priest that would have performed the ceremony is dead. Our marriage will have to wait until I return from Briton once more and we have another in his place,' he says, 'but you *will* be my wife.'

I close my eyes. I do not care why it must wait. For now his words are a chill cloth upon my dread.

'I have spoken with your mother.' He takes my arm and presses his body against mine. 'She tells me you are ripe. That now is the time to create an heir that will secure my claim to the title of king more surely than anything else. No one need know it was conceived prior to a legitimate union.'

I think he will press his lips upon mine. He does not.

He turns his face away from me as he pushes his body against mine and his hair clings to my cheek. It smells of blood and death and the greasy odour of men I will come to recognise. Cold hands, coarse and unkind, cause me to utter a small cry. He does not seem to notice my discomfort; that I try to wriggle from his grasp. He pushes me toward the bed and I let him. I lie down. Tears roll from the corners of my eyes and into my hair. There is a moment of silence and I think perhaps he has gone. Then I hear the contents of his stomach slop into a pan on the floor.

When he has finished, he collapses onto the bed beside me. I wait, knowing he will want to finish what he began. He does not move so I stay silent, hopeful that he is asleep and I can somehow escape this room. I wait, not daring to move for fear of waking him.

A grunt.

He rolls nearer and I scorn myself for not having left sooner as acid and mead linger between us.

'When I return from Briton,' he repeats, 'then we will wed.'

'You have only just returned from Briton,' I say, for our warriors rarely go back across the waters so soon.

'The Bloodshields will leave on the next tide.' His beard, flecked with yellow beads, brushes my chin. His eyes are closed. 'The Britons refuse to pay tribute.'

'The tribute that secures their safety from all of the Irish kings and lords?' I murmur. There are many tributes paid between our tribes and those of foreign lands. Much coin exchanged for reasons some can no longer remember.

He turns away from me.

'Women do not understand the oaths and promises and agreements of men.'

It is as if he forgets what occupied his thoughts moments before. The conversation eases me and I am curious to know more of the tribute our neighbours across the sea refuse to pay. But I am more eager to delay what I know is inevitable.

'My father and my uncles struck the deal,' I say, 'that the tribes of Ireland would not raid those on the coast of Briton if they paid us tribute. I know what was once agreed.'

Morholt snorts.

'Your father was a fool to devote time to telling a daughter so much of what passes between him and his enemies. He would have better spent the time siring a son.'

'Do they refuse to pay because my father is dead?'

'Why else would they refuse?' he says angrily, his eyes still closed, his brow furrowed. 'They do not believe I can guarantee their safety now he is gone. They say your uncles and the other tribes of Ireland will not take heed of my word and the agreement would not be upheld. They would rather pay the tribute to them than to me.'

'What will you do?' I whisper.

Nothing. Then: 'To whom?' His words are murmured and I suspect he drifts into slumber. His breathing heavy between words.

'What will you do,' I say again, 'to those who refuse to pay you tribute … to the Britons?'

I wait for an answer but none comes. His breathing deepens, rhythmic and peaceful, and I realise I am trembling.

I wonder if I should leave now and risk his displeasure should he remember my being here. Or stay until he wakes …

CHAPTER 9

Tristan

The cut on Rufus' leg begins to fester. The physician prods and pokes and applies poultices of varying colours. I am told they will absorb the infection. Draw it from his leg, clean and calm the wound. The smell reminds me of rotten eggs. Rufus winces as the old man presses in, but makes no complaint.

'I have seen the magic of medicine many times,' I say to Rufus. 'My mother once cut herself with a knife and your father's physician worked wonders.'

'My mother was surrounded by them in childbirth,' Rufus replies through clenched teeth. 'And yet she died.'

'She was trying to give birth to a baby the size of a cow. It is no wonder!'

'Do not speak of her like that,' Rufus says, and I know he is worried. Such talk would usually make him laugh.

'All right,' I say, and hold up my hands in surrender. 'No more cow jests.'

'I will have an impressive scar,' he says with a pained smile.

'The women will be fawning over you,' I reply with exaggerated enthusiasm. 'To them you will be known as King Rufus the Brave, with the heroic battle scar on his thigh. They will be crawling over one another to have your bastard offspring. And to the men you will be known as Little Rufus, the warrior with the big fat scar on his leg because he could not move away from a Saxon blade fast enough. I congratulate you, well done!'

Rufus howls with laughter and pain. I laugh too. The physician mutters at the pair of us to keep quiet and for Rufus to stay still until he has finished.

'Will he survive?' I ask the physician.

I glance across to Rufus as I speak. He sleeps now. Fitful and sweating out the infection which tries to take hold. I have yet to send word to his father. I want to ensure Rufus is recovering and that I have positive news before I write that despatch.

'The infection is not too serious.' He nods slowly. An old man from the northern lands, he speaks with a strange accent compared to us southern Britons.

'He will survive?'

'He should live.'

'Then I owe you thanks.'

'Do not thank me so soon. We may yet have to remove the leg.'

I close my eyes as the old man turns to grind and mix more of his healing compounds. I have known men lose a hand and still be able to strap a shield to their arm and hold a sword in the other, and stand in a shield wall with their fellow warriors. But never a leg.

'You know who he is?' My words part warning, part desperation. 'His father will reward you if you save his limb. Rufus is to be King of Kernow one day. The people will think the gods show disfavour if a cripple leads them; if he becomes king at all …'

The old man looks at me with misty eyes, as though he sees all my thoughts and worries.

'It makes no difference to me,' he says. 'King or no king, I cannot change the will of any god, only help your friend along their path.'

The gods, I think. The Christian, the pagan: how they like

to watch us suffer. How they like us to amuse them in their kingdoms as they feast on the courses of our mortal lives.

'Then help the gods,' I say. 'Do what you can for him.'

The next day I ride out with King Geraint to observe the enemy. The bastards stretch the entire eastern frontier. Remains of hasty camps are everywhere; raided villages, merchants telling of sightings. Merchants who trade with the enemy.

The sun is low in a pink sky and the shepherds will savour the day to follow. They shall see their herds more clearly without the mist. Beside me, Geraint rides stiffly. He is not so old, but a hard blow to his chest during the battle, and more than one broken rib, causes him discomfort.

'Do you think Mark will send more men if I ask him?' he says.

I realise now why he asked me to ride out with him. I thought it might be to speak of Rufus. Instead he still presses for more men from his neighbouring kingdom.

'I cannot say, my Lord. We are few enough as it is. Mark has already sent many men to aid Dumnonia's frontier.'

'He has, and I thank him for that. Also remember that I pay for his spearmen and his service. But Mark holds a good many more warriors. He can spare them, I know it.'

I ignore the claim that he pays Mark for his spears, for I know he does not. Geraint wants a number; a surety of how many men can come to his aid. It is not my place to make such promises. I also know that Mark could not promise him more. He is tied to guarding our sea-face, and we have problems enough of our own.

The horses start to whinny. Fog begins to draw in as the sky grows dull and the day cold.

'We should head back to camp, my Lord.'

'The spears, Tristan ap Mark — how many does Kernow have?'

I pull my horse round with impatience.

'With respect, he has given you *all* he can spare. Mark has warriors, it is true, but many of those are seamen off our coast. The rest of our spears keep peace in our country. Yet more defend northern frontiers. He cannot give you what he does not have. If the Irish take Kernow, you will have more than just the Saxon to contend with.'

'Damn it, Nephew of Mark. If Dumnonia falls, Kernow falls too. Or has Mark forgotten what our kingdoms face?'

I bite my tongue at his unfair words. I am here and I fight as I have been asked to, as I have trained to. He should address Rufus or Mark with these requests, not me. Nevertheless I feel myself pulled into the politics of this king.

'You have allies in the north,' I say. 'You will have sent despatches. What do they say?'

Geraint pats his horse. The beast is becoming ever more fractious.

'We have not heard from most of the lords as yet. Those who have replied say all their men are occupied at their own frontiers. They do not understand. We are small and yet we are hit so much harder.'

'Yet their frontiers are larger,' I say.

The day is short. We begin to pick our way back to the camp before darkness falls once more. Geraint holds on to his side as we cross an uneven patch of ground. He grunts in pain.

'I concede, their frontier is larger, but that does not help us.'

I do not wish to speak of it any longer. There is nothing I can do — nor anything Mark can do — to aid further.

'What of Mark's son?' I ask.

A flicker of regret passes over Geraint's face.

'I will arrange an escort to take him back to Kernow. If your king had come himself, instead of sending his son, this would not have happened.'

'I will travel back with Rufus,' I say, ignoring him. 'I need to report back to Mark.'

Geraint scowls. 'And what do you intend to report?'

'The truth, my Lord: that we have been successful so far, but that the Saxon grow in number. I will ask him if he can spare more men, but I can promise nothing.'

That night I return to Rufus' tent. He is sleeping and so I bunk down beside him, pull a woollen blanket over myself. His skin looks pale and clammy and hair clings to his forehead in wet rings. I try not to worry. Instead I wonder what Mark will say when I tell him King Geraint presses for yet more spears. I wonder too how our own frontier holds.

'Tristan?'

Rufus' eyes are closed but he is moving his head as if trying to sense where I am.

'You need rest. Go back to sleep,' I snap.

'It is so cold,' he murmurs.

'I know.' I pull another blanket over him. 'That should be warmer. This is going to be a hard winter.'

He drifts back to sleep. I lie awake as I always do. If sleep could take hold, the hours would slide by easily. Yet I am awake in the depth of night and they stutter and stall as I lie here next to Rufus, as if time does not move at all. I am alone as others are captured by slumber; the only living being in a camp of men who sleep like the dead.

Too many thoughts seethe through my mind: haunting flashes of battle, death strokes grazing my armour, screaming, crying, cursing, wailing … the relief at the end when there were no enemy left and I knew those standing would live another day.

I am anxious to return to Kernow. Mark knows nothing of his son's injury, and even though the Dumnonian physician seems knowledgeable, I would rather Rufus was cared for by our own people. I curse myself over and over for not keeping him as safe as I should have done. He was lucky to survive so many encounters without injury; all those who still remain are. But it matters not. The gods, who revel in chaos, choose our paths for their own amusement and there is nothing we can do to change it. No persuasion or sacrifice can bend their will. No prayers or worship will change their course. Rufus' path is already laid out before him.

Dawn shows itself, and the night seems a long time gone; a week or more. The darkness fades, the light regains its rightful place, and I know I was alone for all of those dark hours.

It is morning and Rufus is dead.

CHAPTER 10

Iseult

I pad barefoot to the doorway and open it with my breath held for fear of making a sound. There is no one waiting outside, and I take one last look at Morholt lying on the bed, the yellow contents of his stomach splattered on the floor and sour breath filling the room.

I want to cry as I rush back to my rooms. Acha sleeps in our bed, turning and whimpering and I cross to a large cabinet on the far wall and run my hands over the doors and in the dark find the key that will open it.

The door swings open and my gowns therein shimmer; the smell of stale fabric floating toward me. I draw it deep into my lungs and stoop down. Part the cloth. Find what I am looking for.

Acha stirs.

I close the cabinet and move quickly to her side and stroke her hair from her face and say: 'Hush now, Acha. Hush now. It is all right. I am all right. Nothing has happened. Sleep ...' I wait a moment to ensure she has drifted back into undisturbed slumber, then leave.

As I walk back to Morholt's rooms, my head is light and my limbs do not feel like my own. I know I must return there even though I do not want to, even though I wish I could slide beneath the sheets next to Acha and sleep all night and wake in the morning and for none of this to have happened.

But it cannot be. I must return to Morholt.

When I enter his room nothing has changed. He lies on his back with his head tilted to one side. I move to look closely at his face. Dark shadows around his eyes flutter and spittle drips from the corner of his mouth and onto the sheets.

I think of spending night after night in this room with him, alone, knowing there is no escape, and from the folds of my gown I withdraw the short knife.

When my father died, his friend opposed Morholt as leader of our tribe. Feidhelm was a man of honour and pride and had served my father well. Morholt had him pegged out over a rock so that he faced the gods and sliced his belly open. The dogs ate most of him, and the rest was left for the birds. He refused to scream even though pain contorted in his face. Our people were told that is what happens to those who do not follow his rule.

My father came to me just before he died. He must have known his men were rebelling against him, and that Morholt wanted his position and his claim to the title of king. He stood in my room and pressed the blade into my hand as I sat on the bed. All he said to me was: 'There are some things in this life we can stop. Others we cannot. Power is dangerous and can only be acquired by taking it from another.'

He left, and two days later he was found dead in his rooms with nothing to suggest the cause.

The blade was a gift from his father. He meant for me to keep it for its value, not its use. I think he wanted me to hide it so that I could keep something of his after he passed, and that Morholt would never find it. If he knew Morholt was going to kill him …

Now I stand before Morholt, the blade clutched in my hand. I am looking at his throat where his beard is tangled and matted and I wonder how I am to pull the knife across it with so much hair and jewels in the way. I have seen men killed. Sometimes they die easily as their blood and life pours from them. Other times they struggle to remain in this world. I know which Morholt will do.

I jump at a faint noise outside, but no other sound stirs and I realise it was nothing.

Lifting my skirts I climb onto the bed and place the knife on the sheets and straddle him. I lean forward to pick up the blade and as I do so his eyes open.

He groans, my stomach lurches, and I pull a nervous smile onto my face as I look down at him.

'Iseult?'

Unsure what to do, I lean forward as though to kiss him, his rotting breath strong, and at the last moment slide the dagger between the sheets. I am not brave enough or strong enough or sure enough to slice away his life now he has woken. He will overpower me, I am sure. And I am afraid he will find the dagger and know my intention, and have me whipped.

Morholt pushes me from him before our lips touch, rolling me back onto the bed. He sits up, lets out a long growling yawn, and staggers across the room. He relieves himself in a bucket in the corner. With my eyes on his back, I fumble for the dagger, to conceal it in my skirts, but the folds of the sheets are a labyrinth in that moment and I cannot find it.

'You are less attractive, Iseult, when you are compliant.' The splashing in the bucket ceases, and he turns to face me. 'You have no fire in you. You succumb to me as you succumb to your mother.'

He nods in the direction of the door for me to leave. The dagger … I pause for a heartbeat, but he is watching me, so I hurry across the room as he takes up my position on the bed.

'Or perhaps,' he says, 'you have more fire in you than I first gave credit for.'

I stop. Dread overcomes me and I cannot breathe. I am facing the door and I feel myself grow cold. Footsteps behind me, then the cold of my own dagger presses against my throat.

Morholt whispers in my ear: 'Your father's?'

Unable to nod for fear of cutting myself, I say, 'It is, my Lord.'

'I remember it. Did you intend to kill me, Iseult?'

'I did.'

He laughs at that and drops the knife from my neck. 'Take it.'

I turn and see that he offers me the handle of the dagger. I grip the long bone handle. He lets go and spreads his arms wide.

'Kill me,' he says, laughing. 'You want to kill me, so *do it.*'

When I do not move, his jovial coaxing turns to anger.

'I did not think so. I would have you killed if I did not want to whelp my sons on you. Your mother should have raised you to know more of the duty you owe your master. And do you know who that master is?'

My face is now covered in his spittle and I feel my hands trembling. Every part of me wants to push the dagger forward, deep into his belly, and watch his life fade away. I hate him for my father's death, for his greed, for his treatment of others, but most of all I cannot bear the thought of his naked body pressed upon mine.

'You are, my Lord.'

'Yes,' he replies. 'I am. I command the warriors. I have the strength of men to rule southern Ireland. And soon I will have a son with the blood of kings of old. Do you understand, you stupid, infantile creature? You are your father's daughter, and that means only one thing to me: your blood is valued more highly than anyone else, and your fertile womb higher still.'

I nod.

'Keep the dagger,' he says, smiling. 'It will make you more interesting as a wife.'

CHAPTER 11

Tristan

I recall how I clasped Rufus' hand more tightly on the pommel of his sword and leant my forehead on our adjoined hands for a brief moment. How bitterness and frustration escaped my lips in a groaning sigh. His face was white and cold. Serene, I thought, in the early morning haze the new day drags.

Now he takes passage with the ferryman. To claim his rightful place in the feasting hall of kings.

We pass markers telling the distance to home. I take little notice as the roads bend and wind their way through forests of oak. A dozen men travel with me in uneasy silence. They are hit hard by our loss and the uncertainty of what will come.

We are in Kernow now, I think. Dips and curves in the ground are familiar. At the head of our company a cart rumbles along the old Roman road. Therein Rufus' body lies wrapped in linen, his sword heavy upon his chest. A box of coins from Geraint to Mark rests beside him. Geraint claims it is a gift. In reality it is compensation for the life of Mark's son. For the heir to Kernow's throne.

I ponder on what will come now Rufus is dead, how our paths in this life will change, anything to take my mind from picturing the look upon Mark's face when he discovers the fate of his son. Mark has a bastard child whom he may put forward as future ruler. Then there is my elder cousin, Oswyn, who rightfully has claim. But Mark's bastard is a sick whelp only twelve years of age who cannot be parted from his mother long enough to learn anything useful. And Oswyn cares more for his own wealth than he does for a kingdom's prospects. In truth I know not what Mark will do.

The nearer we come to home, the more I steel myself for the moment I break the news. Like a coward I thought of sending a messenger ahead. Yet I did not. Mark is like a father to me, and I have not honoured the trust he placed in me. I did not keep his son safe. And I am sick at the prospect that he may not forgive me.

It has been months since I last felt the fresh sea air and heard the crash of waves on our coast. Chill wind bites hard and the never-ending wet fog shields our view of the land so it is doubtful we will see it this day. Feet, fingers and faces are numb as we trudge on. Racing the light. Pushing hard for home.

My body is tiring and I contemplate making camp. But as the last of the sun illuminates the fog and trickles across the beaten ground, horsemen pull out of the darkness ahead. Shimmering black beasts in the distance.

'We are home,' I murmur, recognising Mark's own men.

Elation and resignation pull me apart.

'Tristan.' The first man to dismount nods his head. Leading his horse, he moves closer.

Our party comes to a halt. Rain begins to drum on the ground.

'Eurig,' I say, and embrace the man before me, 'it is good to see you.'

'Gods, you are right about that.' He pulls away with a glance to the sky. 'What are you doing home so soon?'

Eurig is a little older than me. Not a favourite of Mark's with his quick wit and opinionated habits, but a favourite of mine. No man is truly honest save Eurig. He is a man who would spare his last coin for a dead enemy to pay the ferryman, when others would rather take out Saxon eyes with the tip of a knife so they cannot see their fellow men in the feasting halls in which we will all one day gather. In which Rufus waits now.

'I bring Rufus to his father,' I say, gesturing the cart with a tilt of my head.

As we cover the short distance to our fort beside the sea, I explain how Rufus died.

'He wasn't ready,' Eurig says. 'I always said Mark was wrong to let him go east.'

'Would he ever have been ready?' As I speak, I know the answer. It was his fate to die young, I see that now. He was like my brother and yet I know he would never have taken the title of king and made it his own. Would never have commanded men the way his father does, or earned the respect needed to fire courage in battle.

Eurig shrugs. 'Possibly not.'

'What of home? Is all well?'

'Mark is troubled,' Eurig replies, walking beside me. 'No one is safe from his temper. Your mother has refused to speak to him since he sent you and Rufus east, and it will only be worse once she discovers he is dead.'

'She makes a lot of noise, but she means well.'

Eurig nods. 'The Irish king is dead, too, and the man they call Morholt has taken command of the southern tribes.'

'Morholt? I have heard that name.'

'He leads the raiding parties further up the coast on those who refuse to pay tribute. And those who did pay tribute but were too ill-equipped to defend themselves.' He scours the landscape and grimaces. 'A man without morals.'

'Morholt no longer accepts our tribute?' I ask.

'He would accept a tribute. He demanded a tribute. Only Mark refuses to pay it.'

'He does? Why?'

Eurig pats his horse as we pause beside a stream to let the

beasts drink.

'Because Mark does not believe Morholt will honour any arrangement between their people and ours, that the agreement was between the old king and him,' he says with indifference. 'And because Morholt trebled the tribute.'

I laugh at this. The rain is soaking through to my skin, I have much weighted on my mind, and still the outrageous demand tickles me.

'Get greedy and you get nothing.' Eurig gives a smile containing much mischief.

My laughter subsides. 'Except Mark has started a war with the Irish.'

'Perhaps.'

'They do not come?' I wave our line onward. Perhaps half a mile before we reach our beds.

'No sighting yet.'

'They will. And Mark will be ready. He would make no stand if he did not have the men to resist them.'

Eurig bares his teeth and whistles. I hear a call back and realise we are closer than I thought.

'You are jumpy,' Eurig says.

'I have to tell Mark his son is dead.'

'True, but it wasn't your fault.'

'No? I was with him. I could have done more.'

Eurig turns a hard eye on me. 'You never speak with regret, Tristan. Do not begin now. That way lays the path to becoming a milksop.'

I feel myself grow hot. Angry at myself. That a man such as Eurig should see me weak.

'You are right,' I say, although I am not convinced.

'Mark will be angry, no doubt, and he might well blame you, but he will forgive you in time.'

We reach the fort at Tintagel on the north coast. Waves erode the sodden land. The wind is strong and I can barely see as we make the last stretch in darkness. Torches cast shadows long as the cart rumbles along before me.

The fort is an old Roman construction, deserted more than a hundred years. Mark has taken great care to keep the fortifications in good repair. As we are greeted by the lookout, I notice it continues to be well manned in the evening hours.

Eurig calls to several men and the cart, along with Rufus' body, is swallowed into the fort's belly and the gates close protectively behind us.

'Mark will be in the hall,' he says, turning to me.

We step from the darkness into warmth. Men turn to see who has entered. As they realise it is Tristan, nephew of the king, returned from the east and the Saxon frontier, whispers commence and soon silence ends the jovial feasting.

At the farthest end of the hall, thin furs hanging upon a lean frame, Mark stands. As always, there is no circlet upon his head. He wears no warrior bands even though he has earned many. Mild curiosity lifts his features.

'Tristan, you are returned to us? You bring news?'

Eurig strides ahead of me as I close the gap between myself and Mark, and his face turns from one of enquiry to urgent concern, his mouth taut. He inclines his head as Eurig murmurs in his ear, nods, and beckons for us to follow him.

We move to a doorway at the back of the hall.

I can stand in a shield wall, smell the blood of a thousand dead men, feel the blade of an enemy sword twitch across my flesh, yet I struggle to find the heart to tell a man — this man — that his son is dead.

We enter a room with a table at its centre. Not a feasting table, for these are council chambers. This is the place where the men of all the kingdoms of Briton once sat to discuss the invasion of our lands. Now the room is bare and still save the three of us.

Mark walks to the far side of the table and leans with both hands on its surface. His face is weary. He looks to have lived several years in as many months.

'Eurig tells me that your news is better told in private, Tristan. I take it the Saxons—'

'Rufus is dead, my Lord,' I say before he has finished. I can contain the news no longer.

Mark makes no movement. Says nothing. His eyes are dead for a moment, then life flickers back into them and he says: 'Leave us, Eurig.'

'My Lord.' Eurig exits the room without a glance to either of us. He would rather not be here for the king's next words. I hear the merriment of the court and then the door snaps closed and it ceases.

'My son is dead?' Mark asks, another year drawing on his face.

'A Saxon blade. A poisoned Saxon blade,' I add bitterly.

Mark pulls himself up to his full, dominating height and clasps his hands behind his back. 'Were you with him?'

'In battle and at the end.'

Mark nods calmly, as if it is all perfectly understandable — a piece of knowledge from foreign lands, cast before him as a merchant might hint of useless news.

'That is something, at least.'

'It was a scratch.' I am trying to justify what has passed, knowing it should never have come to this. 'I looked at it myself. A clean scratch.'

He moves around the table toward me. Places a firm hand on my shoulder. 'Sometimes, that is all it takes.' His hand slips away and he turns from me.

'Uncle?'

I see his shoulders tense beneath thin furs. Then he lashes out at a chair beside him. It clatters across the floor and his face is contorted in a spasm of pain and anger.

I say nothing. Just stand and watch as Mark stares blankly at the table. What is there to say to a man who has lost his son? I feel his grief. I want to make it dissipate, but I have done more harm than good. I reassured Rufus over and over that confrontations with the Saxons would be like training with wooden swords on a muddy patch of earth, where the worst injury would be to his pride. It was never like that. In my assurance, had I made him complacent?

Finally, Mark walks from the room. I am sure tears glisten in his eyes but he shows no further emotion.

'What do you want me to do?' I ask.

Mark pauses. Looks at me with a questioning stare.

'With Rufus' body?' I say. 'What would you have me do with his body?'

A ghost passes across his face. 'You brought him to Tintagel?'

I nod, confused at his question. 'I brought him home.'

In the great hall the feast continues. I sit beside Mark as he dismisses all food and drink with a wave of his hand. The people know nothing yet of Rufus' death, and Mark seems in no mind to break it to them. Eurig catches my eye. I give a small shrug back, to suggest I know not what Mark is thinking. Rufus' body has been moved to one of the smaller halls not in use.

'When will you tell them?'

Mark does not stir or acknowledge my words. As I give up hope of answer, he says: 'We have more important things to consider at the moment, Tristan.'

'What is more important?'

He lets out a frustrated breath. 'I cannot stay in here. Come and walk with me. The night is damp but quite calm.'

Curious stares follow the king as he rises. Mark takes no notice as we slip from the hall, through the council chambers and passageways I know so well from my childhood. Guards open the door. We step out to face a wall of freezing air. Calm and damp, I think, and bloody cold.

Mark strolls ahead across the wet grass, heading toward the

outer wall of the fort. I take a few running steps to keep up as he springs lithely up the steps to see out across the lands. I follow his solid pace around the rampart in silence, to where the wind draws in off the Irish Sea, pulling salt and spray with it.

'The Irish king is dead,' Mark says, gazing out. 'I presume Eurig has already told you of this?'

'He did.'

'Then you will know too that Lord Morholt has risen to take command in his place?'

'Eurig said he demanded a tribute thrice the size of the one we were paying,' I say. 'And that you refused him.'

Mark rests his chin on his chest for a moment. His grey hair shines in the dark. He is old, much older than I had noticed before. He lifts his head and looks at me.

'Morholt will never leave us in peace. He will raid our coast, send his Bloodshields across from his foreign land and crush us between the Saxons and himself.'

'Do the other Irish tribes stand with him?'

'Oswyn has taken a small boat and heads to the north of Ireland in an attempt to open talks with them. It may be that the northern kings do not approve of this new lord taking lands which were once ruled by one of their own blood.'

'You think Oswyn will be able to open communication with them?'

Mark's smile is almost sympathetic. 'He is a charming young warrior, Tristan. If they are persuadable, he will have no problem on that count.'

The reprimand for my dislike of Oswyn is mild. It is also accurate. Oswyn will be more than capable of persuading the northern Irish to speak with us. Damn him, I think.

'What do we do until we hear from Oswyn?'

'I thought on it much, and made my offer to Morholt.'

There is something in Mark's tone. A resolution I have heard many times before when decisive action must be taken.

He will not be persuaded to change his mind now.

CHAPTER 12

Iseult

There is a sense of relief the morning Morholt departs Ireland, but also the dread of his return as thirty men stride from the halls and across the fields to the shore where one of our many boats waits to be loaded. Our women and children follow, carrying supplies and shouting luck to them, that they come back with the riches rightfully ours. Yet they are not ours. They are the Briton's treasures they try to take; their food and their gold and their livestock.

I wonder sometimes about those Britons, and whether they deserve such plunder. Our warriors tell us they are savages, that they are much like the invaders who take their lands, that their blood is no longer pure but mixed with the barbarian animals of places far away.

There was a man, once. A traveller from Mercia who talked and talked around our fires until he knew everything there was to know of our people. He was older and cleverer than many men, but you would not have known it. He played his innocence well, pretending with wide-eyed looks and naïve questions to be ignorant of our ways and our customs, and yet the tricks he played with his nimble fingers would have us curious night after night. He would have been killed, but he told such wonderful stories about distant countries of which we had never heard that he was allowed to stay a while before he moved on and told others of his adventures.

I wonder now of the men Morholt will kill to obtain the treasures and power he seeks. Will they be men like the Mercian, clever tricksters and storytellers? He had not seemed like a savage to me. Or maybe our warriors are right, and they face wild men across the waters on the large island. Their lands are raided by us and invaded by others. But how would untamed savages have so much gold and silver and bronze? How could they live under Roman rule for centuries and not know civilised ways?

I sit on a flat stone with my chin resting on my knees, Acha beside me, watching the departure. My fear has faded somewhat, knowing I will be able to sleep easy for a short time. I am being given another chance, I think, for the lords across the sea to destroy Morholt, to kill him, so that he might never return to us and take me for his own. How much I cling to that hope and how many moments I imagine the boats grinding onto our shore, and the men walking up the sandbanks to tell us that our leader comes home wrapped in linen, ready to be burnt as we chant prayers to carry him to heaven.

'Your mother approaches,' Acha says, tapping my shoulder.

To my left, Iseult the Elder, my mother, is followed by two servants carrying a chest between them. They are weary, slipping, sliding, struggling. Sudden dread wraps itself around me as I see the chest is my own.

'You are to accompany Morholt,' my mother says. 'I have clothes packed for you.'

I look to the ship being loaded with weapons and food and fresh water.

'To Briton?'

She nods. 'Acha is to go with you.'

I look to Acha whose smile is sympathetic and also fearful. She does not wish to go either.

My mother walks, servants trailing behind her, down to the boat as we dutifully follow. Morholt shouts to his men and makes my step falter, and it is Acha who links my arm with hers.

Mother beckons me onward with a curt look. The sea is heavy and grey, and clouds overhead obliterate the already weakening sun. The waters that were once a comfort to me as I watched the waves skitter back and forth day after day are a comfort no longer. The deep expanse will be my captor until I return home.

CHAPTER 13

Tristan

I feel isolated, the darkness out to sea endless. Feasting, merriment, and Rufus lying in the fort below us forgotten for now. Mark makes no attempt to explain his decision. It is for me to press further.

'What offer did you make him?'

'Morholt will fight our greatest warrior. If he wins, he takes the tribute. He loses, he forfeits the tribute and leaves.'

'Morholt is not afraid of us. What makes you believe he will fight, one man against another?'

'You have not met him, Tristan?'

'No.'

'He is an arrogant man who also needs to prove himself a leader of men. They follow him now, but he will require their unwavering support to maintain a grip on his newfound kingdom.'

'And if we kill him, what difference will it make?'

I rest my hands on the railing which separates the platform from a thirty foot drop. The wood beneath my fingers feels familiar, welcoming, despite the cold and gloom. Mark beside me. Talk of defending our lands and fighting the Irish. Home. Only now Rufus does not stand talking with us. And so I want reassurance before I commit my view on Mark's offer.

'It might not make a difference,' he says. 'There is always

another to rise in a lord's place. That is the way of things. With luck we will find ourselves in a position to make a treaty with the northern Irish kingdoms, and that could give us a good few years of peace. Then we will be able to concentrate on the Saxon front and provide Dumnonia with the support it needs.'

The mention of Dumnonia, and the last support sent — Rufus and me — brings sickness to my throat.

'Peace with the Irish will not come,' I say.

'No, perhaps not peace, but some form of arrangement can be negotiated.' Mark fixes his eyes upon me. There is a sadness, a weakness in them I could almost pity. 'Time is running faster than me now. I remember sitting in council with all the kings of Briton. We attempted to unite ourselves against the Saxons and make a stand against the Irish. We failed in both because the kingdoms could not agree what should be done. They fought over the position of High King, and when that could not be decided upon they argued further on who would therefore lead us, how many spears each lord would provide, how much coin should be given to hire additional spears, who would provide the army with food ... what was fair. Is anything fairer now? We still squabble and bicker. We do not work together. It was fourteen years ago, Tristan. I can still feel the anger and frustration in the room after weeks of talk ... the anger of men who knew we had to come to a decision, to work as one united Briton.' He shakes his head as if he should not have spoken of such matters. 'If I do not try to solidify our position now, ensure our resources are well distributed, what manner of a king does that make me?'

'We should try,' I confirm, once more feeling his reprimand. Ashamed of my doubt. Realising that he does not speak of, or make reference to Rufus. And what will happen now there is no heir to Kernow, even though as he says, time is running faster than him?

'Indeed we should.'

Silence.

'Do you think it will be possible?' I ask.

Tristan

'To make some form of peace?'

'To fight Morholt, just one blade against another, and win?'

Mark claps a hand on my shoulder twice. 'I have confidence,' he says, and turns.

Looking at Mark as he walks away I wonder whether he made the decision to challenge Morholt before or after I told him of Rufus. It does not make a difference; Mark is right as ever. This will be the quickest and cleanest way to resolve the agreement that once held between Morholt's people and ours. This way only my life is staked and not an army of men. Mark knows this. He will also know he gives me opportunity to regain his friendship and respect. To make amends.

It occurs to me now that Mark's decision did indeed come after. That is why I am to fight the Irish Lord. To prove my worth as a man of Kernow, as the nephew of a great king. Or to perish at the hands of a more skilled warrior. To perish as did his son.

I re-enter the hall a while later. Those gathered look from the king seated at the top table to me, and back to their plates and the food I and the other warriors fight to protect. Mark does not acknowledge me. He speaks with his councillors and advisors. Buried in conversation. Planning our confrontation with Morholt.

'Tristan?' My mother looks at me through hopeful, watery eyes. I gather her frail body gently in my arms. Almost feel her breaking under the weight of news. 'Mark has just announced that Rufus is dead,' she says. Words distorted with distress.

I gaze over her shoulder at the people watching our embrace. Every part of me is numb. Her pain was brought by me. Not only did I fail to keep Rufus alive, but I am also the messenger. Bringing my mother nothing but grief.

She wipes her eyes, attempting to disguise the tears, to pretend she does not feel for the loss of little Rufus, the boy she brought up as her own after his own mother passed. How proud

I am of her bravery, of the self-respect evident in the lift of her chin. The hard line of a mouth that scolded us both as children.

'What will Mark do?' she says. 'I tried to speak with him as soon as he broke the news, but he will not talk to me. You have spoken with him. You must know what he plans now. What will happen? Who will become the next heir of Kernow?'

'I do not know.' My words are harsher than I intended. I grip her face in my hands and say, 'I will speak with him further. He has much playing on his mind, Mother. Give him time.'

Time, I think. How we all need time.

CHAPTER 14

Iseult

Acha and I sit shivering, looking out at the grey waves. My warmer clothes, which I sorely need right now, are lying in the trunk below, so Acha and I have to huddle close for warmth. Weaponry fills the decks. Piles of swords and shields and spears and armour. We are the only two women aboard and the men sailing the boat ignore us. I hear Morholt barking orders, see him looking out over the bow, but he has yet to speak with me. Why I have been instructed to accompany him, I have yet to discover.

'Do you think I am to be some sort of gift to the Britons?' I ask Acha.

In truth I am scared that I am being sent to Briton and will not come back to my beloved Ireland, the lands of my father and my family, the ground upon which I played in my childhood. The soil my people have worked for centuries. Trapped on this boat I miss it already.

'He wants you for himself,' she replies. 'And even if he didn't, your uncles would wage war on the south if he sent you to Briton.'

She seems certain; more certain than me. I feel guilty that she has to make this journey with me, even though I know she would have come willingly given the choice. I do not tell her that I took a knife into Morholt's rooms with the intent of killing him. A deluge of fear mixed with a trickle of hatred runs through my body at the memory of his touch and the sensation of his body pressed so closely upon mine, of the sound of him retching. I am both afraid of him and yet powerless to refuse him. In my cowardice I pray that someone else can make my worries disappear.

Acha puts her worn hands around my shoulder and hugs me to her.

'If we are left in Briton, do you think my uncles would come for us?' I ask.

'Oh, my child, they would come if you were taken to the easternmost edge of the old empire, they would. Do not fret.'

Acha lies. My uncles care for their own wealth and their own lands. They have been happy to allow Morholt to rule and I know that if called upon them my safety and happiness would be considered after their own interests.

'Of course,' I say, and smile the same smile I give my mother when I do not wish to listen to her talk of our family's decline.

I watch our people standing on the shore as they grow ever smaller, and despite my mother's temperament, I do not wish to be leaving her. She is one of the strongest people I know.

We sail for what seems like days although the sky has yet to turn black and I know it is still morning. Still Morholt does not speak with me. Part of me is grateful not to have his attention, to pretend as always that I do not exist, but he has me on this boat for a reason, and I will know it soon enough.

The boat rolls with the waves and clouds mass in a dark shadow overhead. Fine rain clings to the hairs on my arms, and within moments the skies erupt in anger and water bounces from the deck and the heads and shoulders of the men who work on. I let it trickle down my face as I sigh because we are heading toward I place I do not know, to lands I have never seen, to meet savages I have never before met. I want time to slow, and yet run faster. Or maybe not pass at all.

CHAPTER 15

Tristan

Mark and I land on the Isle of Samson. The sun is still low and the sea unusually calm. I wonder briefly which way the gods will sway. Do they favour us or the enemy? Have they ceased the rain and wind to watch us as we amuse them, mortal men playing out a game on the hard ground with tools that could no more kill a god than find us peace? How they must laugh at us.

Screeching birds disturb the quiet of this uninhabited stretch of earth. The larger islands surrounding us provide little cover. So far out from the mainland we are exposed. I do not like waiting here.

This is the first time I have stood on Samson's Isle. There is little reason to come here, and it is of no use to pirates or smugglers with its lack of provision. The island is formed of two hills: one south, one north. We land on the north hill. A dozen men in all, though more wait on board ship. Eurig and the other nine warriors settle themselves on the coarse grass. Make a fire to stave off the cold.

'How long will we wait for them?' I ask Mark. He stands beside me, studiously fastening a clasp at the front of his great cloak to stop it billowing in the wind. I notice the armour beneath. He is prepared. He knows that even if I win this fight and kill Morholt, we will likely face the anger of his followers.

'Morholt agreed on today,' Mark replies.

'You think he will come?'

The king looks out across the waters to our right, searching for the Irish boat on the horizon. 'The wind is in his favour so I can see no reason for him to delay. He wants this opportunity as much as we do, remember. I suspect our tribute is more important to him than it was to his predecessor. He needs to pay his warriors and it will have cost him dearly to command enough to gain the position he is in now. If, as I think he intends, he wishes to conquer more lands in Ireland, he needs gold.'

'I had not thought of that. Is Oswyn to warn the northern Irish lords?'

Mark lets slip a victorious grin.

'When it comes to the fight —' I say.

'There is no need to talk of it now.'

I let my impatience simmer for a moment. Mark seems not to notice. I know he is right, that there is little point in speaking of that which is to come. But I want to know in my mind how this confrontation will play itself out.

'Did you speak with your mother?' he asks. The tension between us eases. There is a care between him and his sister, but the bond is not a strong one. He would leave her to dry her own tears in the dark, night after night. He is unable to share precious moments. Moments that would bring them both a little comfort if only he would put an arm about her shoulders and reassure her of vengeance. He cannot admit, even to himself, the feelings of loss which I know haunt him. The same loss that haunts me now.

'I have spoken with her,' I say.

Mark begins to walk along the ridge of the hill. Eurig makes to follow him. 'It is all right, Eurig,' Mark says. 'Stay here and keep a lookout for their boat. I am not going far.'

He continues on, talking, so I sense I am to follow.

'Your mother feels too much for people, Tristan. She must be stronger if she wishes to overcome the great sadness which has found us.'

He is right. Death is something we must all accept. Men die in battle every day. Women in childbirth. Children of sickness that cannot be eased. We feel loss, but we move on, continue life and fight the next battle. Fight more carefully. Am I strong enough to put Rufus' death behind me and make amends? I know I am. It is the guilt which consumes me, the unknown. The forgiveness I seek.

'You are right, Mark. We must all be strong,' I say. 'But you know she cared for him as her own. She cared for him the moment the cord was cut from his mother. She treated him as if he were my brother, without exception.'

I expect a flinch of regret. The stir of a memory at the mention of his dead wife. I want him to show something, but there is nothing as he looks thoughtful and rubs the pommel of his sword.

'Indeed,' he says. 'Perhaps it might be best if she were sent away for a while. She could go to the priory. There she can avoid the talk that pains her.'

I almost choke on my disbelief at his words. He does not understand the simple difference kind words from him would make to her. She need not be sent away. And Mark has never cared which way others pray, which gods they favour. He himself is disbelieving in their powers, swaying toward the Christian God. But to send my mother to a priory, with the Christian monks pressing upon her their pitiful beliefs?

I stop. Look at Mark, my king, as if the monks have addled his mind whilst I fought in Dumnonia.

'She believes in the old gods.' I hear the scorn in my voice, knowing that my uncle will have heard it too. 'She needs us. Her family. She needs to be close.'

Mark nods slowly. 'I have always watched over her, Tristan. I do only what I think is best.'

'Then let her stay in Travena, at Tintagel, with people that she knows. It is her home.'

'Damn it, Tristan, you can be impertinent when it suits you.

Your mother needs to be cared for properly. You know she has not spoken to me with a civil tongue since I sent you and Rufus to Dumnonia?'

'You sent her son and nephew to war. We went willingly. We were both eager to see an end to the Saxon invasion. We did our duty to you and to the people of Kernow. But what did you expect from *her*?'

'I expected her to stand by my decision,' he replies, his voice calm but cold. 'If the king's own kin will not stand by his decisions, then he has little hope of his men doing his bidding.'

'Your warriors are loyal to you. They always have been, and it is not because you pay them,' I reply, stung on behalf of us all. 'You are respected by both your family and your subjects because you are a king. A king that shows them victory and keeps them safe. In war, when have you ever been questioned? When has anyone gone against your command?'

In a low voice he says, 'Never. Not yet. But the day will come.'

Mark shields his eyes against the wind and looks out on the sea with distaste. I do the same. At first I see nothing. Then, where the clouds dip to meet the sea, the dark blur of a boat forms.

'The Irish?' I say.

'I should think so.'

Eurig bellows from behind us. I turn and shout: 'We see them!'

'I do not wish to argue with you, Tristan. Let us walk further. It will take them a while to reach the island and there is something I need to discuss with you before they do.'

Curious, I wait for him to say more.

'You have been wondering what I will do now I have no heir?'

'I think we all have.'

He smiles. A sad smile, as if aware that the people of his kingdom care more for the knowledge of who their next king will be than for his son.

'Oswyn would be the natural choice,' he says, not even mentioning his bastard born. 'There is much to commend him.'

He speaks the name of my cousin as a question. Does he want my approval, knowing that Oswyn and I have never been close? That I could never follow or acknowledge a selfish man as my king?

'You have many warlords in your service, men who would see the chance of becoming successor as an honour. Who would do whatever it took to prove themselves worthy. It is up to you which one you choose.'

Mark listens as I speak, nodding his head slowly. 'I need someone who knows the people of Kernow. I always thought Rufus would fill that role well. He was a caring boy, much like your mother. Too caring, perhaps. He did not display the skills of a warrior, or at least he never appeared to use them. I have struggled for some time to envisage him leading men, and I am aware that others have thought the same. His death, although unfortunate, has saved me from having to make the hard decision of appointing a successor in his place whilst he lived. I have thought on it for some months, and I need someone who is not afraid to make decisions, even ones that would prove unpopular with the people of Kernow, if they were the right decisions. I need someone strong and determined to follow me. Someone who can scourge Briton of the Saxons and keep the Irish at bay when I am gone. What do you say, Tristan?'

I am not listening to Mark fully, thinking instead on his words that he would have replaced Rufus regardless. His own son. A decision a king would have to make. But to be grateful for his death because it avoids the shame that others might witness his admittance of siring a son that the gods chose not to make fit for his father's role, it is a pitiful thought.

Mark is looking at me, awaiting my response with searching eyes.

'I agree. You need someone strong. Oswyn is a strong warrior and I believe he would lead warbands against our enemies as well as he has ever done.'

Mark gives a small laugh. 'You misunderstand, Tristan. I am asking *you* to take the title of king after me. Will you?'

Realisation dawns. Uncomfortable with my stupidity, I look to the ground then out to sea. The Irish are nearer. Much nearer. Fighting Morholt is not only a chance to make amends for Rufus' death. I am to prove myself worthy of succession.

'On one condition,' I say.

'What is that?'

'Forgive me.'

'Forgive you for what?'

'Rufus. I should have done more to protect him.'

Mark pulls a hand through his beard. He looks almost angry.

'Rufus is dead, Tristan. It was not your sword that struck him down and you did not send him to the frontier so incapable of defending himself, lacking the skill to fight as you and my other warriors can fight. I did. Nothing now can change that. Forgiveness is not something you ever need ask of me.'

CHAPTER 16

Iseult

The ragged sea pulls us towards the shore. What am I in all of this? I wonder. Morholt intends to send his most feared warrior to fight for the tribute he wants. Am I therefore not a bargain or token or gesture between their people and ours? Will I return with Morholt to my beloved Ireland?

There are six men and Acha and myself in one boat, and eight men in another. Morholt is wearing all of his armour and holds a shield painted with the blood of our enemy. We are heading toward their land now; to the kin of the men whose blood coats our warriors' shields.

'Morholt, look, they are here,' one of our men says.

At the opposite end of the small island the mast of a ship waves above the low hill like a giant with a rag.

'They will have the tribute with them,' Lord Morholt grunts.

'You will kill them even if they do?' the man asks.

'If we kill them they will not send tribute next year, nor the year after.' I half imagine I see him glance to me as he speaks. 'Use your head, you fool.'

'They should pay a price for their insolence,' the man persists.

'No! The King of Kernow will be on the island himself. Massacre them after they pay tribute and there is no guarantee the next ruler of this forsaken sliver of Briton will be any more amenable than this one. This is the better way. At least this king seems to honour his word. We will win, and he will not break his honour. Our greatest warrior will face the greatest of the Kernish men if they continue to resist us. If they offer tribute, we take it.'

The other man looks as if he would argue with our lord, but he turns away and watches the island.

'You are about to meet a king of Briton,' Morholt says to me. He sneers and I see his teeth, stained with age, and in my mind relive the moment in his chambers when his breath rolled across my face.

The sea is bobbing our boat up and down and up and down and I feel my stomach turn with each movement. I sit silent, attempting to steady myself and stop my head from whirling. Once I know I won't spill my stomach over the side of the boat I look up at Morholt. He is amused by me. To him I am both his future queen and his plaything.

'Which king, my Lord?' I ask, wanting only to break the look he gives me.

Morholt makes a guttural sound and rests his foot on the side of the boat. 'The King of Kernow. Your father should have pressed him harder, as I do now. The tribute he negotiated was barely enough to make the journey between our land and theirs worthwhile.' He leans toward me. 'Your father does not have the chance to press anyone harder now.'

I want to spit at Morholt for his slight against my father, spoken with purposeful cruelty and intention to torment. My father's choices were for our benefit; for the prosperity of us all. Our new lord is not the same man. I am looking into the eyes of my father's killer. A man who murdered his king not only for his lands and position, his wealth and power, but because he enjoys disturbing the balance. He longs to create chaos.

So I say nothing, my lips tight against retort. My words would only prove something worthy of ridicule to him or earn me a blow.

'Kernow's neighbours yield easily to my rule,' he says, watching me as if seeking my feelings. 'They are more sensible men than those of Kernow. This king, though ... this king does not like to play our game. He refuses to give up what he knows he eventually must.'

He is no longer speaking to me, but to himself. The men in our boat growl their agreement.

'I am sure they will kneel to you before we leave this island,' I reply. There is a small satisfaction in my words, answering him as a servant, with restraint, when he and I both know I wish I had a sword like a man to rid the world of his evil soul.

Our small boat grinds on the sea bed as the first sun breaks through the grey sky and pools of light form on the ground. Morholt and his men slip into the murky water and drag the boat onto the land.

'They will do more than kneel,' Morholt says as I clamber from the vessel. 'Kernow will learn to fear us as the other tribes of Briton fear us, when it is their greatest warrior's blood I paint on my shields.'

I glance to his shield and the thick, dark crust upon its surface.

Morholt.

A man who likes watching others suffer. A warlord enjoying the sport of gods.

The warriors of my beloved Ireland fasten their sword belts and pull on their helmets. How any man can be more fearsome or more skilled in slicing away the lives of others, I cannot imagine. They are my kin, and yet I do not feel a part of this group of people standing on the shore of a country I find so unfamiliar.

Green swirls of water catch at my feet. My sea. The same nature that clings to my own shoreline and beckons me home. And yet the wind and waves sound hollow and detached. The sun shines, but it is a stark and unkind light that filters between clouds. Untrodden grass grows coarse between stones and rocks. A lonely and cruel nature resides here. My people were right; only savages could live in such a desolate place.

Acha says nothing as I loose my grip on the crook of her arm and use both of mine to balance a path to the grassy slope a few paces away. We scrabble up the banking and fall behind as the men bound to the top. We follow the curve of the land, skirting the crevices where it has fallen to the sea, making for where we saw the other boat's mast above the hills.

'My lord?' I am slightly breathless and my head feels light from the ascent, but it is only a moment before brisk air fills my body.

Morholt does not answer me, pacing quickly ahead. Uninterested in anything I would say.

'Lord Morholt?' I run a few paces to close the gap between us. 'Why am I here?'

'We are here to claim what is rightfully ours.' It is as if he believes this country and the riches it contains are his, that they belong to him without question.

'And me? Why am *I* here?'

'What is the purpose of victory if there is no woman to witness it and tell of her man's greatness?'

I walk on, following this man, our lord, my future king, and despise him for his vanity. What man requires witness of death? Surely the very fact that he has killed another leader of men should be enough?

'See,' Acha says. 'There is no malice in his bringing you here, is there Iseult? And we will both return home as soon as this is over.'

Home. My lands and my sea and my wind. The elements that Morholt, even if he is godlike, cannot control. That is why I feel at peace with them, because they are beyond the choices of men.

CHAPTER 17

Tristan

By default — the absence of another son — I am the heir to Kernow's throne.

I have power now. More than I anticipated acquiring in my life. I had wanted a warband, the ability to pay men from my own purse, lead them in defence of our country. Now? What now? It is as though a title which is not yet mine has changed me as the seasons change the land, yet with no certainty that summer will come again. Could I be a better king than Oswyn or any of the warlords of Kernow? For the good of our people, for all of my beliefs, I think I could. Yet it is not what I wanted. I am not that man.

Many think there is little difference between warlords and kings. Kings are often forged by accomplishment in battle, and I have seen success in my short years; it is why Mark sent me to the frontier. But few men find the following kingship commands. Fewer still desire the strain of the politics associated with the title. I know, even now, I am one of the latter.

'Will you, Tristan?' Mark asks. 'I need to know now whether this is a position you are certain you are willing to accept. I will ask these men to bear witness to my choice of successor.'

'I can be whatever you need me to be. But Oswyn will not look kindly upon it.' My reluctance is clear. Would I rather have Oswyn rule than do so myself?

'I realise that, yes. It is one reason I am grateful he is in Ireland as we speak. If your position and rank is established before he returns, it will ease the new order of things.'

Well said, I think. The new order. As the youngest nephew, I am chosen as the king's first. It unsettles me. I do not like change.

We turn and walk back to where Eurig and the men stand waiting. They are restless. The Irish ship has landed on the far side of the other hill, and the lord of the Bloodshields will make his way toward the strip adjoining our two small warbands.

'Do we go to meet them, Lord King?' Eurig asks. He is not nervous. Eurig is conscious of danger, he is aware of repercussion, but he is never nervous. He wants an end to this matter between us and our enemy. A swift end.

Mark answers: 'In a moment. First, I need you and the men —' he nods to those whose attention is rapt as they listen, '— to witness my wishes. You all know my son Rufus is dead. It is to be known that I name Tristan, my nephew and a leader of men, as heir to Kernow's throne when I enter heaven or set sail with the ferryman.'

The men nod, as if they had known it. Perhaps they had. Thinking now, it was always Oswyn or me. If Rufus had survived, the security of the throne could never be assured whilst our cousin lived. Oswyn will certainly attempt to take it, even now.

I look into the men's faces. I want to know if this news is welcome to them. I have no wish to rule over men who would prefer another lord. They nod solemnly, giving me no further clue as to their desires. Even Eurig fails to show the kindly look of a friend and mentor that would ease me.

We walk down steep slopes toward the thin stretch of land between the south and north hills. I see flecks of movement. Mark is beside me. He is dressed in armour dull and worn. As though he feels we are defeated before the first clash of iron has even rung in the gusty air. The weight of my own sword is heavy on my hip. With every step it feels heavier. There is not the same battle-frenzied rage when you fight a man alone, just the sickening feeling that you must kill before you are killed. That you must do it in order to live.

Mark pauses at the neck of the strip of dirt. As do the Irish.

The sea wind howls the excitement of the gods.

'Let us be done with this,' Mark says to me, or to himself. I cannot tell.

He heads toward our enemy. A confident stride. The rest of us follow.

I try to look like the warrior I am. The man who has brought down hundreds of the blonde Saxon scum with the very blade that rubs against my thigh now. With each step, I grow smaller. The Irish are a dozen men, as are we. Two women huddle in fear behind them. A tribute to us? I doubt it. An offering or a temptation, even a distraction, perhaps.

'They bring women,' I say.

'They can bring whomever they wish, so long as it is no more than the warriors agreed. It makes no difference to us,' Mark replies.

We stride our half of the gap. A warrior's step. Eyes locked on the enemy we would rip through with a blade. These are the moments in which to instil fear, and I wonder which side looks most fearsome. Which side the gods favour.

CHAPTER 18

Iseult

My face flushes with heat. Worsened because I can feel it, the rapid rise of blood in my neck and cheeks and the inevitable glow my white skin takes, even in the cold. The Britons glance at me and Acha with disapproval. Perhaps they know I am here to witness the victory Morholt is convinced he will have, or because they think I am an offering, but not attractive enough to tempt them. I wish they would look away.

I am unsure at first which warrior amongst these Kernish men is king. They are all dressed simply; barely any warrior rings and shining plunder strapped to them. Their armour looks sturdy and their shields are neatly wrapped in leather and painted with a red-beaked chough; a much less intimidating covering than that of my own people. Even though I do not know these men, they appear not to be as fierce and wild as our warlords of Ireland. Their posture is defiant, but not aggressive. They are a calm people who stand against their enemies, but will not win. I pity them for their misguided defiance and almost wish I had a chance to plead with them to pay the tribute and return to their wives and children before it is too late. Morholt's victory on these shores will be an easy one. Of that I am certain.

'You choose to bring tribute, King Mark? Or do you choose to forfeit Kernow's greatest warrior?' Morholt asks the question with a pleasure that reminds me of the way he spoke of my father. If they did not enjoy watching this entertainment, the gods would surely smite him. I secretly wonder at the emotion I might experience were he wrong, and the Britons proved victorious.

One of the Kernish men — a man who is as plainly dressed as the others with nothing to indicate his authority except an obedient silence from his companions — glances to the ground for a few moments, then raises his head and says: 'Passage across the waters to join those gone before us will be two gold coins. That is the same for you as it is for me. Every tribe, be it Briton, Saxon, Irish, needs land for its people to work and live on. Anything more is greed.'

The leader of the Kernish men reminds me of my father, the way he speaks plainly and concisely, as if every word spoken ought to be obvious and accepted by all, and yet I know Morholt is thinking he is little more than a fool who pays too much heed to ideals.

Around me, I feel the prickle of excitement as our warriors realise the Britons will not give up their gold as easily as Morholt believed and that without the riches, swords will be drawn. I wish the Britons would yield, so that I might return home before blood is spilled.

'A king? You are a king of Briton?' Morholt laughs. I feel embarrassment on behalf of those standing before us, for my lord's cheap humour. 'Your kingdoms fall to invaders because you lack ambition, *King* Mark. No enemy fears a leader who cannot lead.'

The men either side of the King of Kernow — this man they call Mark, who appears no more a king than I a queen — look as if they move closer in their anger at Morholt's words, but they have not stepped a single pace. One of the men, a man much younger than the king, who holds all the impatience of youth in his determined face, rubs the hilt of his sword with his thumb as if tempted to draw it and finish in that moment what has already begun.

Finish this, I think. Let the uncertainty of these two groups of warriors facing one another be over. Or let one side yield to the other.

'I lead my people to a life without threat. You are a thief, a common raider,' the Kernish king replies. 'That is why we find ourselves on this island. You thought I would give you gold so that you can return and demand yet more, season after season? You have no honour and I believe no tribute could ever be agreed and kept between my people and yours.'

Morholt does not rise to this king's tone. Instead he takes a further step toward the Britons and they bristle, their hands twitching to sword hilts and their faces alert, eyes suspicious. I admire them both, I realise. My Lord Morholt comes to a foreign land and has no trace of apprehension at demanding his desires, and these Kernish men show not one measure of nervousness in standing against him.

'You make the wrong decision,' Morholt says.

'One fight, sword upon sword, to the death, and the future price of peace between our kingdoms is decided. That is what was agreed.'

The king of the Britons does not even offer our passage back to Ireland, never to return, and I know he has resigned himself to seeing through the bargain that was made. And for the first time I am afraid of what will happen to Acha and I if these Britons prove to be more capable with a sword than I first thought ...

I look at the line of men before us and wonder which lean warrior will face my lord thinking he can win. The man little older than myself who rubs the hilt of his sword catches my eye and something of resignation passes over his face. His eyes are pale and hard, but they appear to be apologising for what will come, for this whole meeting and the death which will follow, and it is clear this is the man who will step forth to fight for his king on this sliver of land.

His gaze moves from me to my fellow Irish, weighing each of us in turn, and I wish he would look back at me so I can see reassurance in them that all will be well no matter the outcome. The Kernish king is waiting for my lord to respond, but Morholt is a man who likes to make others wait, teetering on the edge with anticipation.

'I never pass on an invitation to draw blood,' Morholt says. 'And the blood of Britons curdles like the cowardly. Better for my men to paint their shields.'

'Your acceptance is welcomed.' The young Briton speaks for the first time and his words send warmth through me to contrast the cold wind. His voice is clipped and short and has no fear to it. I am surprised that his king shows no indication of annoyance that one of his warriors has interrupted the exchange, and I think perhaps they are father and son.

The young warrior flashes me a hard stare. I am frozen, then realise that a smile plays on my lips at his words and my lord's supposition. Stood behind Morholt, I cannot see his face, but I expect he thinks I grin at what he believes to be stubborn, inexperienced foolishness from this Briton. Yet the young warrior's arms are laced with the signs of battles old and recent, and his words I believe were spoken with satisfaction and not hot-headed anger. He is a man not only of words.

And for the first time this day I feel a curiosity, and something of excitement.

CHAPTER 19

Tristan

The girl is smiling at me, at us. Arrogant and amused, thinking her lord a better man than any of ours. It is the way of the Irish, to assume their superiority above all others. To think they can come to our shores and threaten. And now they bring women to taunt us as we fight for what is ours. Taking advantage of our weakened position as we face other enemies that have crossed other seas. Watching as the blood of men is spilled because of their greed, seeing men's bowels loosen on the earth as they die. Will they enjoy it as much when it is their own lord's piss soaking our land?

Their leader grins. A wicked grin. A man who will draw his sword with enjoyment and not one fragment of restraint. I despise him even more for the fear that begins to seep into my veins. Making my heart pump harder.

'You like a challenge, boy?' he says.

Boy. Morholt might match Mark's age, but he knows I am no boy. He will have noticed my shield, the beatings taken by Saxon axe these past months. He will know I am younger than he is, but I have seen my share of battlefields. How much apprehension is there in a man who looks as confident as he?

'I would like the chance to drive my sword under your ribcage,' I reply. 'And watch your innards slither down my blade.'

'I will cook your flesh over a fire on your own shore,' he says.

'I hear Britons taste of pig.'

'And I have heard the Irish taste of shit.'

Mark takes the smallest step forward. I say nothing more, knowing Mark is not angry with me, but also that he does not care for the hot words that pass between warriors when they are readying for a fight.

'Now we have exchanged the customary insults, are you prepared to draw your sword for the tribute you want?' Mark asks Morholt.

'I am ever ready.' The sound of Morholt's sword sliding from its scabbard causes all the men in our group to reach for their blades. My own sword breathes a hiss of excitement.

Mark alone does not draw his weapon.

'Lower your sword, Tristan.'

Confused, I let the heavy iron tip drop to the ground.

Mark unclips his cloak and hands it to Eurig.

'What are you doing?' I ask.

'Settling this matter of a tribute and earning the respect of all the Irish kings. This has gone on long enough.'

As tall and lean as Mark is, this is not a fight he can win.

'You said I would fight him?'

Mark's expression is blank. 'No, I did not say that. I told you he would fight our greatest warrior. What greater man can an Irish lord fight than a king of Briton?'

I think back on our exchange. Know that my name was never uttered when he spoke of the fight. And curse myself for my own idiocy.

Embarrassed, I turn my back on the Irish and mutter, 'And what if he kills you? What then, Mark? Your son is *dead*. Your life holds no less value because of that. Is that why you wanted to name me as your successor? Because you think you will die on this island on the edge of that Irish bastard's sword?'

'It was a decision made before I knew of Rufus,' Mark says, his voice beginning to rise. 'Question the decision of a king when it is your own and not before.'

The words hit my face like the punches Oswyn threw when we were children. All hatred and shame as I lay on the floor, boyhood pride willing me to struggle to my feet. I hated him for it.

'Do as you wish,' I say, though my voice is low and I half hope he does not hear me. He seems not to, for he says nothing and continues unbuckling his sword.

She is watching me. The girl with the pale hair and pale face that is almost lost in this bleak weather. She makes me uncomfortable. I am a man, a warrior, yet her stare, even in its innocence, makes me check myself. Perhaps she is a witch.

'Let me fight him.'

'I will not speak of this further.'

'Then tell me why?'

Mark drops his sword-belt to the ground.

'Because a dead man cannot blame himself.'

CHAPTER 20

Iseult

Question the decision of a king when it is your own and not before? So this young warrior I see is the son of King Mark, and will one day become a king himself. No wonder he can speak to his lord in such a way and not find himself under the heavy earth upon which we stand.

I do not hear what more is said as their voices dip and the wind rages. Yet it is the older man who passes his cloak to another, unbuckles his sword belt and unfastens the iron plate protecting his chest, and steps forward to face my lord. And there is something of resignation in his eyes that compels pity. This, I know, is a man placing faith in whatever gods he looks to.

Morholt hoots with laughter.

'You fight me yourself, Mark? Will you hold a shield, or do you need a free hand to grip a stick to keep you upright as you wave your sword at me?'

I study King Mark, but nothing of him says he needs any assistance. He will not win, of that I am sure — his blood will soak this ground as the waves lapping the shore soak the sand — but his tall, lean frame, unencumbered by armour, and his assured step tells me he will not make this an easy fight for my lord.

'If you die on the edge of my blade,' King Mark says, 'your men and your women are free to leave this island and return home.'

I question whether to believe his words, but I know they are true. Everything of this man tells me so: his desire to protect his kingdom and his words of greed and honour. And I am drawn to the man who would think them.

'I pity the fools under your rule, Mark. For their king is a weakling. A bow-legged creature of a defeated island that cannot see its own cock for a fat belly hanging in the way.'

King Mark inclines his head, unwilling to argue the point or trade insults as we stand in the wind. I do not mind the cold, but I feel Acha shiver beside me.

'If you die,' Morholt continues, 'I will have your queen as part of the tribute you owe me. I will bend her over the milk-stool you call a throne.'

'Do not listen to his poisonous tongue,' the young warrior says.

His advice is not necessary, as the Kernish king does not flinch at my lord's words. Perhaps he does not care for his queen; I know Morholt does not care for more than my womb and my blood. Or perhaps King Mark is sure his queen is safe in a guarded castle on the mainland, away from this place of blood and misery and threat that I have been brought to.

The King of Kernow slides his sword from its unbuckled scabbard and seems to feel the balance. I have felt the weight of swords before, and the ability of those who wield them during battle or a fight surprises me.

The warriors of Briton take a pace backward, and Acha and I do the same. Our warriors hold their position and it is Morholt who walks forward to meet King Mark and his own blade is drawn and ready to take the tribute he so desires.

'I will see you next in the feasting hall,' King Mark says.

'Meet me in a Christian hell, for I am already at one with Lucifer.'

Morholt has his back to me, but I can see the Kernish king's face. It is aging and tired and it is calm. I notice the calm most as he raises his shield and takes my lord's first strike upon it: a loud thump that sends me another step backward so that I almost trip over Acha's feet. She huddles me to her and I watch as Morholt throws another strike at the Kernish king. And I feel myself willing King Mark on. *Fight him*, I think. Fight back. Do not just take every blow for eventually one will be the last.

The two men watch each other. Waiting to see who will strike next.

Kill him.

Kill him and save me from his bed and my duty as a daughter of the blood.

Kill him so that I might return to my beloved Ireland a free woman.

Kill him.

'Kill him.'

Acha's tightened grip tells me I have said the words aloud. Iron scrapes against iron. The heavy thump of King Mark's blade on my lord's blood encrusted shield rings out. Sweat or fine drizzle runs down both men's faces and they grunt with effort and there is silence from the rest of us. King Mark's son, the young warrior, looks past the pair of fighters to me. All I can see in his face is loathing and I do not understand why.

Rain begins to patter on the ground.

The drips bounce as they hit the wet earth and I look away from the fight and to the unhappy sky. Water splashes on my face and I welcome its chill on my skin. I do not want to see what is happening. I cannot watch. Let it be over and my fate be known.

CHAPTER 21

Tristan

What goes through Mark's mind? Fighting because a dead man cannot blame himself? Perhaps, but I can blame him for his kingdom being without a king, for leaving me to take charge just moments after he has proclaimed me his heir. Does he want to die? Has Rufus' death addled his mind? Has he lost all reason? Surely he knows he is not the fittest man amongst us, or the quickest. And he has given his promise to let these people return to Ireland should he kill their lord. I am unsure how wise those words are. Just as I know I will not hand over any tribute to this man with his painted shield even if Mark should fall.

Mark weighs his sword in his hand. A short sword. And I know he trusts it.

He moves as I would move. We were trained by the same sword-master. We trained together. He has taken Morholt's first strikes on his shield and now they circle one other. Mark's step is steady. His expression has changed from boredom at the insults exchanged. Now his brow is creased in concentration. Mouth tight with determination.

Morholt's sword crashes into Mark's shield again. Mark backs from him, taking the brunt of each blow with his arm and shoulder, sparing his sword. His right knee begins to buckle under the impact. And I look on. At any moment he will break the tirade of this Irish lord's bludgeoning metal and will meet him with his own blade.

My breath catches in my throat.

I drag damp air into my lungs as I will Mark on. Knowing a few more heartbeats and it will be over. Wanting to make each strike myself. Itching to hold that sword for him. Willing Morholt to falter. For conclusion to be swift.

'Mark must win.'

I reply without looking at Eurig. 'He had better, or we will all be wading through shit back home.'

I hear a shout. *Kill him.* Beyond Mark and the Irish bastard I see the girl with the pale hair and paler skin. The look of desire and enthusiasm for Mark's defeat is repulsive. She screams for the death of a man she knows nothing of. If I were fighting her lord she would be shouting those same words. Does she crave the death of all Britons in this way?

My focus returns to Mark. I worry the words have penetrated his concentration, but he shows no sign. His short sword plays fast. But the length of Morholt's blade means he cannot come close to puncturing the bastard's flesh. Mark is calm in his defence; Morholt grins, foreseeing the death of a king. Thinking that we will perish should Mark fall. That we Britons will die on this forsaken island. Our island. Killed on our own ground. At the hands of men who want to plunder a few gold coins. With their women watching and cheering at the sight of their lord hacking and cursing at a king. Bringing death upon us.

And I watch. I want to drive my sword through their ribcages, swearing to whichever higher being rules over kings that I will renege on Mark's word and kill every last one of them should he fall.

Rain pummels the ground, gods spitting on the mud, at a fight that can bring them no more entertainment than me pleasure. Mark brings his shield up horizontally and Morholt's blade slides across the surface, gouging a deep track in the painted chough and then Mark's face. Blood sheets his cheek, mingled with the spittle of the gods.

Mark loses footing, slides on the mud and stones. He groans in pain and surprise. My stomach lurches as Morholt pulls back his blade to bring it down.

Mark rams the edge of his shield into Morholt's chest. Winded, an involuntary moan leaves him. And I see the dull sheen of my king's sword whip round and crash into the side of his head. Morholt's eyes roll in confusion, anger, and the disbelief of a warrior too confident of his own skill. He falls backward with a satisfying squelch in our mud, moaning and writhing on the slippery ground.

Mark slumps beside him. I unsheathe my blade and wait to see what course the Irish warriors will take now their lord has fallen. One starts toward us. Teeth bared. Eyes wild and remorseless like those of the Saxon. But the rest do not follow.

'I will gouge your eyeballs from your skulls,' he shouts. 'I will cut out your tongues so that you can never utter the name of my lord. I would skewer your balls on my knife if they were large enough …'

As he talks, I walk toward Morholt and kick his sword from his hand. Whichever god he might worship, he can do it as a mortal and not a warrior as we are. Then I spit on him. Mark would not approve. He thinks that even the enemy should be treated with a respect I cannot give. Then I drive my blade into his throat, breaking his neck as I do so.

The warrior charges towards me in a frenzy. I lift my sword from Morholt's throat and arc it round, bringing it low, cutting into his legs and he falls.

The other ten warriors turn and run.

Back to their boats.

Back to Ireland.

CHAPTER 22

Iseult

A strike from a king and a second from his son, and my Lord Morholt lies on the ground with blood pooling around him.

'Dear gods,' Acha says.

She clutches me, as if providing comfort, whereas I think she yearns for comfort herself as our warriors desert us on these foreign shores. I am aware that we are two women amongst these Kernish men. I do not know what we should do. We could follow our warriors but they will not wait for us if we fall behind. Do I believe that King Mark will honour his word that we should live if Morholt fell?

I realise in that moment which king I trust in most. Whose people I am drawn to.

I pull from Acha's grip and look steadily at the king's son who has slain my lord as I walk to where King Mark kneels in the mud, clutching his face. The young warrior makes to approach me, and so keeping my eyes on him I say to the King of Kernow: 'Let me see, Lord King. Let me look at your face.'

'It is nothing,' he says. 'Nothing at all.'

I manage to tease his hand away and see the cut is far enough from his eye not to have damaged his sight. But the wound is deep, and I am sure his cheekbone is shattered.

'You need a physician, Lord King. It looks as if the bone is broken.' I take a rag from my skirt pocket, fold it, and press it gently against his face. Beneath the blood he is almost as white as my hand.

'I will see a physician when I am home.' He looks at me, his eyes focussing on me for the first time and I feel conscious of my hands upon him; that tending his wound has not been well received. I should have waited until he addressed Acha and me.

He clutches the wad of cloth and using my hand for assistance, pulls himself to his feet.

'It looks like I am still the King of Kernow,' he says to his son. 'But my choice still stands. You will remain my heir, Tristan.'

And now I am puzzled. Would not this young warrior, Tristan, already be the king's heir if he was his son? If he has been chosen, then is he a younger son, or no son at all?

'What is your name?' he asks me.

'Iseult, Lord King.'

'And your companion?'

'My maid, Acha.'

'Your maid?' His voice is steady but he knows already I am no servant girl or slave.

I take a deep breath and say as confidently as I can: 'I am King Donnchadh's daughter.'

I await his response, growing more nervous because he is looking at me without a word, and all eyes are upon me.

'I was sorry to hear of your father's passing,' King Mark says eventually. 'We had an agreement, your father and I, one to which your Lord Morholt was too greedy to adhere.' The king looks down at Morholt's body. 'He can stay where he fell. If your companions wish to return for his body when we have gone, they are welcome.'

'And us?' Acha says, her voice uneven. 'What of us?'

'As King Donnchadh's daughter, she will fetch a high ransom,' Tristan says. 'Or fair terms when you negotiate the treaty.'

'You suggest taking her back to Tintagel?'

'Until an agreement has been decided with her family. It would be the obvious course.' Then in a low voice he says, 'The north of Ireland is ruled by her uncles? Whom Oswyn talks with now?'

King Mark's eyes flick to me. I nod confirmation.

Then Tristan says: 'Even if you do not ransom her, the kings of Ireland might consider our leaving her here as disrespectful if her people do not return and she should perish.'

'True.'

'We do not yet know the politics of Morholt's rule. Or how much ground Oswyn will succeed in gaining. We should play our pieces carefully.'

Mark murmurs inaudibly. 'You are right. They come with us to Tintagel.'

I could weep for the blood in my veins. Blood that brought me here, blood that could see me safely home.

CHAPTER 23

Tristan

The old woman looks fearful, and the girl appears concerned for Mark. She cries out for his death then wipes the blood from his cheek as I have seen his sister wipe away the sweat of fever. The girl is tender. Caring. She shows a natural concern, not a nicety born of fear. I was confused by the women's presence before. Now I am more so.

Walking back to the boat the women are ahead with our men. Mark and I drop behind at his indication.

'Morholt could have killed you,' I say, seeking something more of an explanation.

'He could have killed anyone who chose to fight him,' Mark replies. He still holds the wad of cloth to his face to stem the flow of blood.

'It should have been me. I wanted to face him.'

'Why should it?' Mark's voice is sharp. 'Because you felt you had something to atone for? If I had fallen to his sword, you would be king, but if you were killed, Kernow would remain without a successor. The people of Ireland will know he fell to a king of Briton, and we will have their respect. They will fear us now, if only a little. It was the obvious choice, Tristan. Do not allow guilt to overcome your judgement. The right decision is not always the one you wish to make.'

'There is still Oswyn. Even if I became king, he would be

my natural successor until I produced an heir of my own. And we would have the respect of the Irish lords no matter who had fought Morholt.' My argument is a feeble one. I know Mark better than he thinks. I can feel a sense of satisfaction roll off him. Having spent his whole reign longing for peace, he has won the fight that matters.

'Oswyn is not my choice. And you will have sons soon enough. I do not wish to talk more of this. What I want to discuss is the girl.'

The girl, the daughter of an Irish king, glances back at us. She appears concerned. And so she ought to be.

'What of her?'

'Donnchadh died a few months past. I have heard rumour he was poisoned. If this is true, and Morholt had a part in it, then it may be we are in a better position with the northern Irish lords than I had hoped.'

'Now he is dead.'

'Yes. An alliance may well present itself. What the girl is worth remains to be seen. When her father was alive, she would have been prized greatly by her people. But now?'

'Our position is strengthened with Morholt's death. Not because we have the girl,' I say, realising the truth. Damn it. Why is nothing in this life simple?

'Without knowing the exact politics of her people, we cannot be sure.'

I feel uneasy about the whole situation. The problems we face taking her back to Tintagel, and the supposition on the part of the Irish lords prove problematic, and yet …

'Will you send her home?'

Mark pauses. 'Home? No, not yet. We have no idea what we would be giving up. We need to speak with her first, see what she can tell us of Ireland's powers.'

'And what she was doing here.'

'Doubtless Morholt had his reasons, however senseless.'

Yes, he will have had his reasons. Whatever they were, he is dead now.

I smell the rain, wet grass, the salt breeze, and reflect upon our victory. Yet my spirit is as damp as it was this morning. I still feel the presence of Rufus, though I sense the empty space created by his absence.

Mark draws air through his teeth. 'It is always better when you survive a fight without injury,' he says. He looks at the blood on the cloth then presses it back to his face.

'Was the girl right? Do you think your cheekbone broken?'

'Likely, yes. Nothing to cause any worry. It is just a scratch.'

My legs suddenly feel as if they cannot support me. My stomach swims. I recall speaking those same words to Rufus, believing them to be true, knowing now they were not.

'What troubles you, Tristan?'

'Nothing.'

The journey home is quiet. No laughter, whooping or chatter. No basking in the death of the Irish lord. Just the rain hammering on the deck. The women sit in shamed silence. The girl as straight-backed as anyone can be when they are a captive travelling to a foreign land.

Sea winds drag the boat along the coast. Colour fades from the horizon, the water and the faces of those around me as night falls. Tintagel Castle becomes clear in the distance. I conjure an image of our halls to stave off the cold. I look at the girl, this Iseult of Ireland, and wonder how she will find my homeland and our people. She turns her head slightly as if sensing my gaze but I do not look away. Everything tells me she is the enemy, born to a race that raided our coast for a hundred years and more. And I find I resent myself for giving concern to what she might think of me and mine.

She turns fully and rests her eyes upon me and smiles. An expression filled with warmth. And to my surprise I return her smile.

CHAPTER 24

Iseult

My stomach swims with nervousness on this boat with strangers. But even so I feel safer than I have felt since my father's death. Does the King of Kernow realise what he has done for me? I am compelled to thank him, and promise myself I will make my gratitude known, that I will do my utmost to see him rewarded for his actions as hot tears threaten to tumble.

Looking across the sea to our destination I feel the eyes of the Britons upon me. My cheeks grow warm and I resolve to continue looking out and pretend I do not notice. My curiosity is strengthened by my pull toward these people, and eventually I turn to see the young warrior, Tristan, looking at me and smiling. It is reassuring and I feel myself relax as any uncertainty ebbs away. I smile back.

We reach the mainland and I see the monstrous building of stone that must be the Kernish stronghold. It rises from the rocks, daunting and fierce. Lord Morholt called these people savages and I supposed them to live in squalor, but I see they do not. I make sense of it now. These people on their island are falling to invaders just as Morholt fell in the fight between him and King Mark; they are people and they are not so different from us.

King Mark orders the men off the boat and we trudge towards the castle. Acha slips on the mud and before I have chance to double back to help her, Tristan curls his arms beneath hers and hauls her up.

'Watch yourself,' he warns, 'we have had rain for weeks.'

'As have we,' I say as I wait for them. 'Rain enough to drown a thousand men.'

I realise the stupidity of my words, speaking of drowning men and the implication that I might imply I wish it of those who killed my lord. I want to tell him that is not what I meant, to correct myself, but I find the feeling of stupidity increases.

'You look half drowned yourself,' he replies.

For a moment I am taken aback, before I realise he jests. We both chuckle. These Britons, it seems, are an easy people with whom to speak.

Acha pulls her arm from Tristan's grasp and plods on. As the laughter ends I hear the sky hum, promising rain. I think of walking along the shore in Ireland, savouring the feel of water on my face and the freshness of the air, and by contrast the comfort of a warm blanket when I returned home. I think of it, though I do not yearn for it as I had. Curiosity of this place and its people interest me in a way I never thought they could.

I take hold of my skirts and increase my pace up the embankment. Acha is on one side, murmuring curses at the physicality of the walk, and Tristan strides easily on my other side.

'Who are you?' I ask.

'Who?'

'What is your place? You are important amongst the Kernish people?'

'I am a warrior.'

I grin. 'That is a little obvious.'

Tristan glances at me but it seems my jests are not as well received.

'You and King Mark, you appear close.'

'I am Mark's nephew.'

It makes sense now, why he and the king are at ease with one another. Then he says with a wry smile, 'Perhaps I do look like a warrior, but you do not look like a princess.'

I laugh, long and without restraint; forgetting everything. Tristan looks a little unsure and I regain myself.

'My mother always said I looked like any one of the girls in our tribe. Even so, I have never been called a princess amongst our people. A woman of the blood, the daughter of a king, the errant girl who walks the beach at night and would rather live in the wild than with my people, or simply Iseult. But never once a princess.'

'If you looked more like one, they might.'

'With my hair coiled and my skirts not so dirty?'

'You'll not have clean skirts walking in Briton.'

I lift my chin and look at him and say: 'Holding my head a little higher than the common people? As if I desire to be liked and respected as a superior when I have no wish to be either?' They are all points my mother has made many times, always wanting me to act more as she does, more like a future queen.

Tristan's face is unreadable and I think perhaps I have gone too far, that our exchange has become too serious. Perhaps I offend him.

'None of those things,' he says.

'And so what does one look like, warrior of Kernow?'

'A lot less beautiful.'

CHAPTER 25

Tristan

My compliment is light. A gesture to ease the girl. I expect her to laugh, but she does not. The evening is gloomy, yet I know she is embarrassed by my words. I am not. I realise I speak true. She is something … unexpected.

Her wide eyes no longer meet mine. They flicker ahead and to her maid. Reflecting the last light, her discomfort. She is right, her hair is not coiled, hanging loose and tangled. It is an unkempt, uncaring presence. I take in her appearance. A bright face. Eyes unsure and observant. An expression of intrigue adopted when at ease. And I know she is more beautiful still for her banter. Her humour. Her ability to both charm and offend in a few words. The smile I cannot help but share.

The enemy.

I should ask of her family. The uncles whom Oswyn speaks with as I walk beside their niece. The niece of kings as I am nephew of a king.

I go to speak, but cannot order my words.

'It is hard, to lose your lord,' I say at last.

'To lose a lord or be a captive?' she asks.

'Both.'

She shakes her head. 'You know as much of our people as I know of yours. I was told you are savages.'

'And what do you find?'

A playful smirk.

'Why do you want to know what I find hard?'

'It is a pleasant way of asking your position. Whether you were wed to Morholt. What your value is. If your uncles would see fit to pay a ransom for you, or negotiate a new treaty. In what situation your people find themselves now their lord is dead. All things you will be asked when we reach Tintagel, whether you wish to be asked or not.'

She looks scornful as she replies. 'Your king does not know what he has saved me from. However I am treated by your people, it will be nothing to being the wife of Morholt. I had longed for his death.'

Kill him.

'And to my uncles I mean little. I once thought they cared for their blood-bonds, that if my mother and I called upon them, they would see Morholt as a traitor. But he raided and he ruled and caused them no trouble. I thought that all our people hated Morholt, for his cruelty and because he killed my father, but we are — we were — much wealthier under his rule. And so I realise now I was the only person to mourn my father. Even my mother is more concerned with her own position and interest to spare a thought for him.'

'Are you sure Morholt would not have been seen as a traitor if your uncles knew he had killed their brother?'

She shrugs. 'My mother does not believe so.'

'Mark has sent men to speak with them,' I say. 'Before he and Morholt agreed to fight. To see if they would curb your lord and honour the terms of our treaty.'

She nods and looks at our castle scraping the heavens. What does she think? That we should have paid the tribute because we could? Because we do not live in squalor as she presumed? Even in her hatred of Morholt, does she think her people entitled to the tribute we once paid? Who am I to need the satisfaction of that knowledge; to know what she thinks of us? She is a child of the Irish and she will return to them.

Mark casts a casual glance over his shoulder. He will no doubt wonder how forthcoming the girl is. What kind of a peace might be found. Not knowing that the girl, if she speaks the truth, is worth less than a piece of Saxon scum.

'What will happen to us?' she asks.

I see her maid look intently at me. I falter. It is not my choice what happens, perhaps not even Mark's. It will depend on the Irish kings and their decision. Do I say more empty words, more worthless assurance to her as I did my friend?

'I have no way of knowing.' I watch her as I speak. She already knows I can give her no answers. That there are no answers to be had. We live in a world where the only surety is that promises are made and broken.

The day is almost snuffed out. My eyes strain against the dark. We are picking up pace and the castle is close. The girl Iseult is quiet beside me. I can think of nothing to say either. It matters not. It is an easy silence; as familiar as scouting the Dumnonian frontier with Rufus.

We reach the castle. My mother runs across the courtyard to greet us. She takes the wad of cloth from Mark's cheek and I hear her gasp. She presses the cloth back and kisses his other cheek. Then she falls into a clumsy embrace with me. She is shaking. I feel the damp of her cloak and know she has stood on the ramparts waiting for our return.

'Calm, mother. There is no damage done.'

She whimpers and gabbles into my shoulder. 'Do not leave again, Tristan. I cannot bear it. Please do not leave again, my son.'

I stroke her wet, braided hair and hold her tightly. When she is ready, I let her go. She gives a small sigh then turns to the two Irish women.

'Welcome to our home,' she says as brightly as she can. 'My name is Isabel.' She does not know them. There has been no introduction, but that is the way of my mother.

The two women dip into a curtsy.

'No need for that, my child,' my mother says. 'Come inside and we shall find you food and warm, dry clothes and chambers. They will be with us for a while, Mark?'

'For now.'

'Come then.'

I know by the way my mother puts her arm on Iseult's shoulder that she has adopted herself a daughter. She is a mother to all lost souls, and I think how alike the two women might be.

CHAPTER 26

Iseult

Acha and I are given separate rooms and yet we stay in the same bed on our first night with the Kernish. I know as I lie on the soft mattress that I am no longer afraid. I wonder if my mother worries for me. Whether she knows more than I did of the Britons across the sea and trusts I am safe and well.

I think of King Mark and his bravery, facing Morholt and the wound he has suffered. I do not know what will happen to Acha and me, whether we will be returned to Ireland. But I think no harm will come to us in this castle on the coast of a land I had once thought savage. It was our men who were savage; I see that now, the great castle stood proud and strong against the sea-storms raging, holding wealth my people desired. I wonder who will command the men of my homeland now Morholt is gone, and whether his men returned to the island to take his body home. No woman will taste the stench of his breath or his rage, no man will feel his blade tear them in two, and for that I am thankful.

And I think of the young nephew, of Tristan. I think of the way he caught Acha as she fell and his jests, and of his wanting to prove himself against Morholt. He is a troubled man, I know. I sense his mind does not rest easy nor does sleep come to him. I think of his eyes staring at me as our lords fought and his thoughts no longer interest me. I find myself instead searching my own memory for the colour of those eyes that watched me. My mind lingers on the way he held his mother and stroked her hair, offering her a comfort I remember my father giving me. I imagine his firm embrace, the sudden safety I find myself in tenfold, and I am there in his arms as I drift into undisturbed slumber.

I wake to sunshine pouring through the thin windows of our room and I wonder if the gods favour me this day, if the fine weather is an omen to precede a new life here in Kernow.

Acha is already awake and dressed. She is folding and sorting and hanging.

'What are they?'

'A gift, from the king's sister.'

I crawl sleepily from the bed and stand beside Acha to inspect the gifts we have been given. The dresses are beautiful. Isabel's own? I am not sure. To whomever they belong I am grateful to have something to wear, for my own clothes are soiled and torn and wet from the day before and many days of sleeping beside the sea.

'We should be careful of the gifts we accept,' Acha says as I step into a gown she holds for me. 'We are not guests here, we are prisoners.'

'We are not treated as prisoners, Acha.'

'That may change.' Her mouth is stern and pinched so that her lips wrinkle as if sucking something bitter. How wrong she is.

We are escorted through the castle and to a room where a small fire burns in a hearth, despite the spring day. There is a table and a dozen or more chairs, and I sit as close to the fire as I can, for my bones are still damp-cold. Acha stands waiting. She does not feel as comfortable as I, not knowing why we have been called to wait in this room.

A few moments pass and the king himself enters. I stand quickly and curtsey, and he ushers me to sit, that there is no need for such formalities. He sits close to the fire so that there is barely an arm's reach between us, and I look at the wound on his face. Small, neat stitches tie the cut together, and I wonder whose precise hand it was that tended him last night. I am responsible, I feel, for he saved me, even though he would have fought Morholt whether I was present or not.

'My Lord, I must thank you —'

'Finding chambers fit for a king's daughter is not worthy of gratitude. You have my sister to thank for the clothes she has found for you. My late wife would approve, I think, that her gowns were put to use.'

I see sadness glimmering in green eyes and I will a tear so that I can wipe it away as I pressed cloth to his wound, and feel suddenly conscious of the fabric which skims so perfectly my body. He is watching me, or perhaps he sees his dead wife sat before him. I want to speak but I am unsure what to say, to feel.

'I will thank her then, when I see her next.'

The king appears to stir from a trance.

'I must understand your situation in Ireland.' He glances to Acha. 'It is important we know what we face and how amenable your uncles in the north of Ireland might be to another treaty. My nephew already discusses terms with them, but they will not yet know of Morholt's death. They did not support him, I think?'

King Mark desires peace. His voice, the softness edged with hope and desperation tells me so. He wants to spare his people the raiding Morholt subjected them to, and I cannot blame him. He must know, too, that I can offer him little. My knowledge does not extend to the desires our northern kings may have. They did not come south when my father was killed. They offered my mother and me neither hope nor protection.

'I am afraid, Lord King, that I can offer you no insight. Lord Morholt was a man whose greed preceded all else. I had thought my uncles would protect us, but we have heard nothing since my father's death.'

'Iseult ...' He seems unsure of himself. A man, I know already, who is always sure of everything; as the sun rising and setting and the winter that will see the weakest of his kingdom perish. '... you were married to Lord Morholt?'

'I was not.'

King Mark nods, and I look at his hair, almost black and combed back from his high forehead. His cheeks are sunken, as if slumped in a chair after a day's work in the fields. His hands rest gently on his knee.

'I will wait for my nephew, Oswyn, to return from your uncles in the north before taking any further course of action. I fear you must suffer our damp halls and Kernish food a little longer. You have everything you need?'

'You have already been more than kind.'

'You are no prisoner here, Iseult. Either of you,' he says, looking to Acha. 'You are free to come and go as you please.'

Free to come and go as I please, he says, and I feel tears forming a hazy film over my eyes and my throat tightens. Does he know, this man, this king, what he gives to me? A freedom I thought I would never have. I cannot speak.

King Mark does not wait for my response. I may cause him discomfort, I think, and he stands and leaves the room without another word. And I am left alone with Acha. She comes to me and holds me as she knows the relief I feel, that at least, for now, I am safe in this castle of our enemy. Our enemy. I laugh into Acha's shoulder at that. She pulls away from me.

'What is it?'

'We are being treated as queens in our enemy's castle and lands,' I say.

I see a rare moment of relief spread over her face also and I know in that moment no matter what happens from this time forward, we will stay in Kernow.

And never return to Ireland.

CHAPTER 27

Tristan

Mark waits and so do I. Mark because he wants an end to the Irish feud, to know what news Oswyn will bring with his return. I wait because the presence of the Irish girl unnerves me, causes a sense of dread.

She sits in the great hall each night. Her smile brings merriment to those around her. Her hair shines silver, no longer tangled with mud and seaweed and salt-damp. I see her cheeks rose under the gaze of our men. When I watch her too long my heart grows heavy and I think of Rufus; drifting out to sea, flames defying the water upon which they dance. Iseult's laughter has replaced his. Her light makes others forget. But my heart is torn. Her innocence can never bring Rufus back across the lake with the Ferryman. He is waiting now in the feasting hall. I see him. Laughing just as Iseult does now, joking with the men, causing the cheeks of the women to warm.

I sit, thinking of Rufus and Iseult with barely a thought for my future reign over Kernow. I wonder how serious Mark is. Was his decision spurred by fear of defeat when fighting Morholt? I see the men, they look at me differently. I am no longer simply the King's nephew. One day I will sit where Mark sits now, and know I accepted the throne only because I want to save our kingdom from Oswyn's rule.

Mark smiles. The only time I have seen the sorrow of losing

Rufus lift since I gave him the news. Iseult stands and walks to the harp in the corner of the room. She has told Mark she plays, and when she sits and her hands touch the strings I hear music to rival the larks' voice in the forests as I silently wait for deer or Saxon enemy.

The hall falls silent. When she has finished everyone erupts with applause. She has become a source of entertainment to our people. They watch her. Every man in the room is becoming infatuated with her. Mark is still smiling as she takes her seat. He too is under her spell. It is why I will not approach her, or take the time to know her better. She is a being from another world, and to the Irish coast she will go. That is what I dread: her departure which will surely come with Oswyn's return.

Three days and no sighting of a ship bearing my cousin. I long for its approach so that the girl with the silver hair will return to Ireland. I find myself drawn to her. She lingers on my every thought, and yet I spoke with her only briefly on her arrival to our lands.

My mother wishes to visit the priory and I am to accompany her. The skies are bright and calm as I saddle the horses ready. My mother worships the old gods of Briton, but even so her sympathies to the orphans cared for by the sisterhood see her take food and coin weekly to ease their suffering.

I wait for her by the castle's forge, watching the rhythmic beating of iron and feeling the heat of the coals on my face. I see Rufus in the glowing embers. The blood from his wound. And I hear his voice as we spoke to one another in our tent each night, alone.

When I look up I see not only my mother approach, but Iseult too. I curse inwardly. She will ride with us to the priory. A good half day round trip.

'I thought Iseult might join us,' my mother says.

'The brothers will need to take confession after seeing Iseult,'

I say. I realise a moment too late the words I have spoken. My mother pretends not to have heard, but Iseult will not meet my eye. I realise they are words Rufus would have spoken.

I call for a squire to saddle another two horses.

'I had not thought we would ride,' Iseult says quietly to my mother.

'You do not ride?' I ask. I am shocked by this news. Remind myself she is the daughter of a king. She would have always ridden in a cart, not upon horseback.

My mother says: 'She can ride with you, Tristan.' And I feel greater dread than standing in a shield wall. I am sweating and have lost the order of my thoughts.

Iseult waits as I take the reins of my horse and guide him across to her.

'I will lift you up.'

She is in front of me. Her eyes downturned, the long, fair lashes resting on her cheeks. I take hold of her waist and she grips my shoulders. I lift her easily into the saddle. The horse moves under the weight of his rider, but before I can soothe him she is already stroking his neck and he calms.

I mount behind her, loop my arms either side of her waist and take the reins. We set off and her hair flutters in the breeze. I smell camomile and lavender. She is tense, I notice.

'Relax, he is friendly enough.'

She rides side-saddle, but looks ahead. As I think of her, what thoughts occupy her mind? Is she restless to be back amongst her own people? Is she still afraid of us, even after the days she has spent in Kernish company?

Others' company, for I have offered her none.

Is that the cause of her unease? Her silence? Am I a cause of fear?

'What do you make of our country?' I ask.

'It is as wet and cold as Ireland.' I sense the smile in her voice. The ease with which we spoke on the shore when she first arrived on our coast.

'Do you spend much time out in the wet and cold?' I curse myself. A foolish question.

'I sleep on the beach at home.'

Her voice is light. I wonder if her words are a jest.

'I hope you sleep outdoors only on dry nights,' my mother says, 'if Ireland is as wet and cold as Briton.'

The horse treads rough ground. The motion causes Iseult to lose balance. I take the reins in one hand and grip her waist with the other. She tenses, but after a moment her body relaxes against mine and the thought of her in my bed enters my mind for a heartbeat. I dismiss it. She is a girl from Ireland; a daughter of a king. I should not encourage nor harbour ideas of her, not when she is to return to Ireland. Not when her safety here could forge a treaty to end war with the Irish and see us a hundred years of peace.

She turns and glances at me. Blushes. Her eyes are so blue as to be almost violet.

'Isabel is a kind woman,' she says, her voice low so that my mother does not hear.

'She likes to impress guests. If only you knew her better ...'

'Ah! You mean she is like you?'

'Me?' I feign offence and laugh.

She turns her head and looks at me again. This time there is no embarrassed moment as our eyes meet. She raises a brow, smirks.

'I am glad to be of amusement,' I say.

'You are a natural.'

'That I am. I once pleaded for the position of court jester, but Mark would not have it on the grounds that I cannot juggle or play the lute.'

'But can you dance? That is the question.'

'Of course I can.'

'Well?'

'Dreadfully.'

She laughs, and through her laughter says: 'Then you are the perfect jester. The poorer the dancing, the better the act!'

'Then it appears by your low standards of court jestering that I am qualified.'

'You are, if only you could escape your future as king, your dreams could be fulfilled.'

'I could wear the hat, king or not.'

'You would still need to polish the bells as you would need to polish your crown.'

She is laughing hard now. At my expense or her joke I do not know. I do not care. I like that she is laughing with me. Her mood is the lightest I have seen, and her humour is much the same as mine. Much the same as Rufus'.

'I did not expect the welcome we have received here.' Her voice is serious. Her tone one that does not invite mocking, but I have no control over my words.

'If we sent you back to Ireland battered and bruised, there would be no treaty.'

Iseult does not reply. I have offended, I am sure.

'Will I go back to Ireland?' She asks as if she does not wish to return.

'Mark will see you safely home.'

'Ireland is no home for me,' she says. 'I was at home with the sea and the sand and the shingle of my shores, with the salt spray in my hair.'

'And you will have them again.'

She turns from me. Her body is tense once more and wish I knew her thoughts.

'We share the same shores,' she murmurs.

CHAPTER 28

Iseult

Darkness lingers in the priory as it did in my Lord Morholt's chambers. The scent of incense drifts on the cold, damp air even though the day outside shines hot, and candles fight to illuminate the corners of this vast place. I do not hear what the priests say, nor the hum of prayer or the soft steps of the sisterhood. Tristan's voice is in my head. Swirling and curling around words that are becoming familiar to me. *Amusement* and *dreadfully* and *jestering*. I long to hear him say my name, and wonder if I might laugh as he stumbles upon the lilt of it.

He is walking beside his mother as we follow a priest, glancing back at me now and then, smiling. Reassurance? Friendship? I am not sure. I do not care. His face, his smile, his eyes. I wish to study them more closely and for longer. To trace a map of the shores upon him and feel skin on skin the warmth I felt through his tunic as we rode.

Does he suspect my thoughts? Can he know that I am thinking of him now? When he looks to me again I feel my cheeks grow hot and I am thankful then for the dimness in which we walk.

I have never thought on my appearance, how I look, the gowns I wear. I am a creature of the sea and the sand and the shingle of the shores. I detest the need to dress the part, to comb my hair and be a king's daughter. It has brought me no pleasure in the past to appear well groomed, but now I am conscious of my walk, my hands, the shape of my face and the movement of my lips. Each part now moves of its own accord. I am no longer in control of a collected self.

We have stopped. Tristan and I wait as Isabel is led into a room. She is to confess and I wonder does she see the way the priest looks at the coins she carries, the ones I think she always brings with her.

Tristan sits upon a bench as if this place were as familiar as his own home. He has been here many times I think. A weekly task, this visit. We are alone. More alone than we have ever been with the priest gone and the hall quiet.

I look about me, but the only seat is on the bench beside Tristan.

'Sit down,' he beckons. And so I do. We are not as close as we were when I rode with him, but still the distance feels less.

'Your mother comes here often?'

'More so since Rufus died. She used to come to see the children and bring coin and food for them. I did not know she now confessed.'

He speaks the name of Rufus evenly but his disguise of the pain he shares with his mother is clear.

'Rufus was the king's son?'

'And my mother's nephew.'

'What happened to him?'

He seems surprised by my question and appears reluctant to speak, but after a moment he says: 'He died fighting the Saxon in Dumnonia.'

I keep silent, for I think he has more to say and I am eager to hear his words and be the ear to aid his grief.

'I knew before we ever left Kernow that he was no warrior.'

'You could not have stopped him, I think.'

He looks at me as if I understand little of this world. That I was not there and could not comprehend the loss he knows.

'I could have,' he says. 'But it would have been a blow for him, to know that his father and I did not think him, the king's son, fit to fight in battle. I am unsure if I should have found the courage to do so.'

'You do not lack courage, of that I am certain. You would have fought my Lord Morholt had your king not been determined to do so himself.'

'I would have, you are right. I owe Mark everything I have. He has given my mother a good life, raised me like his own, given me opportunity to become a warrior. Now he has named me his heir. Of that I do not know what to think. It should have been Rufus. I take his place yet I all but took his life.'

I see his hurt but I have no way to relieve it. There is no bandage to cover it or compress to soothe. He must live with his guilt and his sorrow until it is light enough to bear.

'I am glad you did not fight Morholt,' I say.

'Why is that?'

'He might have killed you.'

Tristan grins and leans back on the bench and says with confidence: 'I am the better fighter.'

'Of King Mark or Lord Morholt?'

'Of both, of course.'

'Had King Mark not defeated Morholt I would be his wife now.'

'A prospect you did not cherish?'

I smile at him and the need to ask me this question. I had always thought my feelings at the prospect of marrying Lord Morholt were obvious.

'Does wishing a man dead make you the worst of men?' I ask.

'Of women, you mean?' he says, smiling.

'Of women, of people, yes. Does it? I wished Lord Morholt dead many times.'

'I think he was a man any god would excuse you for wishing dead.'

'Each time Lord Morholt travelled to Briton I prayed that he would not return. I asked each and every god to take him away and bring my father back. They have granted me the former and now I wait for the latter which I know can never come.'

Tristan's expression becomes grave, and yet I feel lighter having said the words.

'Morholt killed your father?'

'He poisoned him, I think. I know.'

Tristan takes hold of my fingers and squeezes them.

I look down at our hands and know that this man, this Tristan, is a good man. His guilt and his fears make him so and I know too that for a moment our sadness is lifted by the words we have spoken and shared.

He lets go my fingers and runs his hand through his hair. It is lighter than when I first met him, rain-soaked and dark.

'You call Morholt *lord* even now.'

'He was a man to be feared.'

Silence. I am thinking of Tristan's fingers upon mine. His questions. The openness with which we talk as I can talk with Acha.

'I do not wish to return to Ireland,' I say.

Tristan looks at me, as if weighing my sincerity. Perhaps he does not believe Kernow is a country in which anyone should wish to stay with Saxons harrying their lands, but a new chapter has begun and I feel there to be a place for me here in his court.

'It is for your uncles and Mark to decide whether or not you return to Ireland.' His voice is guarded, careful. Does he not wish me to stay? Is there no room for a girl from across the sea in this land of Britons? Am I no better than a Saxon? I had thought I felt the warmth of wanting but it seems I did not.

Isabel emerges. Her face is wet with tears and her sad eyes pull at my heart. She looks first to me and then to Tristan, as if she knows every word we have spoken and I feel exposed. Isabel is kind and caring and she is observant, I think. She has deduced from two expressions an age of conversation.

Why, suddenly, do I feel I have something to hide? The heat creeping into my face betrays me and I cannot look at Tristan. My mind and my heart are a wave crashed into rocks, scattered and sprayed.

'Are you ready to leave?' Tristan asks Isabel.

She nods and we walk to the stables where our horses are being fed.

We set off back to the castle. I am tired yet I am not. My body is exhausted but my mind is running away of its own accord and I cannot rein my feelings and thoughts.

Not a word has Tristan breathed since our departure. His body is pressed against me, his chest against my back, and I feel safe; much safer than I have felt since my father's death. Unspoken words I do not know rest on the tip of my tongue, unwilling to take flight. I think of our jesting earlier, but I have little humour in me and now is not the time.

We pause beside a beck and the horses drink. Isabel is tired, I can see her eyes heavy and I know she wishes to lie down. It cannot be far now, I think.

'Do you wish to rest, mother?' Tristan asks.

'I am fine,' she says, but I know she is not.

'I would rest, Tristan,' I say, his name awkward on my tongue.

He dismounts and helps me down and then his mother, and I see her relief at our pause. She sits on a tree stump by the beck and bathes her neck.

Tristan loops the reins of the horses over a tree branch and silently gestures for me to walk with him. We pause out of Isabel's hearing.

'You are kind. My mother is not a stubborn woman, but she is embarrassed to admit when she feels weakness.'

'It was no trouble.'

'Iseult, did you mean what you said? You wish to stay here in Briton?'

My name on his lips. How I savour his perfect pronunciation

and softness with which it is spoken. I will him to say it again so that I might bathe in the sound.

'I do.' I want to add *with you,* but do not. I am drawn to him but I am afraid of acting foolishly. I do not know if he feels the same, or what the reason behind his reserve might be. Is he afraid, as I am?

'I shall speak to Mark,' he says. 'It would depend on your family, but Mark might know of a way for you to stay in Briton should you want to.'

Words seem lost to me. I do not know how to thank him for what he has offered, for my life to be lived here in Briton amongst a new people. Away from my homeland and the people I no longer know, the men who saw my father dead, and my mother who is empty and broken.

'You would not mind our staying here?'

Tristan laughs.

'Of course not. Why would I mind?'

I shrug his question away. Perhaps he does not mind because he cares little either way.

We walk back to the horses and mount. Isabel looks more tired than she did before, her hair grey in the dying light. We ride carefully and I am pondering so many thoughts and visions of a future on these shores. What would happen if I stayed, I wonder. Would Tristan want me as Morholt had wanted me? Would it be to secure his position as King of Kernow, and an alliance with my uncles that coin could never buy? A woman of the blood. I remember it as suddenly as if I had tripped upon it. Which man would ever marry me for me and me alone when the blood of Irish kings flows in my veins? What escape am I to find from my history and my fate?

CHAPTER 29

Tristan

We approach the castle. The sun hides from the day and mist begins to rise. My mother is unwell. Her distance is greater than when I first told her of Rufus and I wonder what the priests said to her; what portents they have conjured for her nightmares.

If I ask Mark whether Iseult can stay in Kernow, will he have any power to make it happen? She is a prisoner on our shores. A future queen of Ireland and in no future can I see her uncles allowing her to reside here. What would Mark say if I confessed of my attachment to an Irish girl? Would he think me stupid? Compassionate? Lustful? Then it comes to me. A light so blinding, so warm, that I can do nothing but bask in it.

A new treaty. Forged with blood.

I feel Iseult against me. She is no longer tense. Her body has relaxed against mine and I dare myself to think that she enjoys the pressure of being pressed against me as much as I do. I can no more let her leave than I would have let Rufus die if I could have stopped it.

Excitement fills me as I think on my words to Mark. This is why I have been destined to Kernow's throne; to allow me this chance. I will tell Mark of my proposition; to agree a unity between Iseult and myself, an alliance between the Irish and the Kernish secured with marriage.

I drift into my own world. It is brighter than before. I forget the Saxon and the field of blood, death and mud in Dumnonia. My aching for Rufus does not disappear, but it eases. Our enemies seem far away if they exist at all. I think of my bed and I think of Iseult beside me, her silver hair on my pillow and the sons and daughters she could bring. I had thought life began with a sword in your hand, but now I know it begins with this bond for which I cannot find words. We do not speak to one another, yet our silence is comfortable.

I am lost in my thoughts and do not realise that with my arm wrapped around her waist my thumb strokes her stomach with a longing of years rather than days. I notice only when she places her hand over mine.

I help my mother down from her horse. I do not think she has seen the intimacy which has passed between us, and does not comment upon it. She kisses my cheek, then Iseult's, and leaves, her expression heavy with sorrow and troublesome thoughts. I am torn between staying with Iseult and ensuring my mother is well. I choose to stay.

Now Iseult and I are alone again.

We are stood in the castle courtyard. The sun has disappeared. We are illuminated only by the echo of the day and it lights Iseult's hair so that if you breathed it might fly like a dandelion gone to seed. Should I take her hand in mine, I wonder. I want to, but I am unsure. I do not wish to make promises I cannot keep, or utter words of assurance for fear of shattering the dream. I must speak first with Mark.

'It is late. I must ready for dinner,' Iseult says.

'You can find your rooms?'

'I can.'

I nod and turn to leave.

'Tristan, wait.'

She looks confused. Lost, even. Am I the cause?

I step closer, put my hands upon her shoulders and kiss her

forehead.

She smiles at me and I leave her then. She does not say my name again nor halt my departure. I had thought to wait until tomorrow before seeking Mark, but I am compelled to talk with him this night.

I walk the halls determined. The thought of waiting until after we have eaten to gain audience with Mark is unbearable. I know that he can give little assurance, even if he agreed to my proposal, but I am compelled to speak with him anyway.

'Tristan!'

Eurig runs to catch up with me.

'What is it, friend?'

'Oswyn has returned from Ireland,' he says. 'Mark asked me to find you.'

I double back and we make our way to the council chambers.

'What news does Oswyn bring?'

'The kings of Ireland know of Lord Morholt's fate. They are open to a new truce. That is as much as I know.'

'That is good news.'

'You would not think it to look at Oswyn's face. I must warn you, Tristan, he knows of your being Mark's heir. Tread carefully, your cousin is not a man you want to make an enemy of.'

It is the first mention of my becoming heir that Eurig has made.

'He will be an enemy either way. We have never agreed on anything.'

'True. But you should not antagonise him.'

'Me?' I half laugh and Eurig smiles.

'You have not made mention of Mark's decision. You are always a man of opinion, Eurig, yet you do not have one now?'

Eurig weighs me. Then says: 'It was I who told Mark to make you heir. Rufus could never have been king, we both know that.'

'You spoke with him of this before Rufus died?' My voice has risen.

'You asked my opinion, Tristan, and I have told you. I thought Kernow would do better under your rule than any other man after Mark.'

My anger slips away. I shake my head.

'I am grateful for your confidence, Eurig.'

I open the door to the council chambers and look upon my cousin for the first time since the balance of power shifted. Many claim Oswyn and me to be twins. We are the same height, our long, rectangular faces angled with symmetry. We are the same but for our hair: his is dirty and yellow, mine is dark like Mark's.

He looks at me as I look at myself when I think of Rufus' death, with disgust and anger.

'Safe journey?' I ask Oswyn.

'Tedious. Talks with the Irish always are. I hear our cousin Rufus died fighting at your side.'

I resist the urge to draw my sword and instead ask Mark:

'What say the Irish?'

Mark appears positive in his expression and almost joyous. Surely the Irish cannot have proposed a treaty so amenable as to lighten his mood? Then I glance at Oswyn and know from the humour laced with his hatred that he plots against me already.

'The Irish kings learned of Morholt's fate whilst Oswyn was at their court. It seems he was a common enemy, allowed to rule for a short time only because the northern Irish had yet to muster a force to quash him. Now that Morholt is dead, the northern kings will send a force to either encompass Morholt's remaining supporters, or defeat them. One of Donnchadh's brothers will move their army and rule the southern kingdoms.'

'What of the treaty?' I ask.

It is Oswyn who answers, his voice taunting. 'The old treaty and tribute will stand. As a gesture of goodwill, the Irish kings offer the hand of Donnchadh's daughter to Mark, Kernow's *king.'*

His emphasis on the final word is unmistakeable, but I barely take note. The daughter of which Oswyn refers is Iseult. My head feels light. Sickness overwhelms. I need Mark to understand that if she is to marry a man of Kernow, it must be me.

'Mark, might I speak with you?' I find my voice is not as loud and sure as I intend, but he hears me. I note Oswyn takes a care to watch me.

'Of course.' He turns to Oswyn and grips his shoulders. 'You are a good man. I am proud of you. I have named Tristan heir to my throne after me, but I think no less of you. No man could better serve.'

Eurig serves better, I think, and it pains me to realise he is still in the room listening to the words Mark speaks, knowing as he must that he is as equal in loyalty and skill as Mark's other nephew.

Oswyn and Eurig leave the room. Mark and I are alone. As I attempt to form words, Mark speaks for me.

'I know what you are thinking. She is Irish and I never expected a daughter of Ireland to become a queen of Kernow, but I feel it is a good solution; a benefit to the future. Might I be open with you, Tristan? This could be our chance to secure the peace I have longed for my whole life. Peace with the Irish, at least. But it's not just peace with our enemies I crave, it is my own.' He pauses. 'I find the nights cold and my years are advancing more quickly than I had ever imagined. It is a long time since Rufus' mother died.

'I fear I burden you. I have named you heir and could yet take that away from you. Iseult has little choice, of course, on the fate her uncles have chosen for her, and I would never force her to a marriage she wholly refused, but I would like to think there is some affection between us, if only a certain respect.

His words are a sour wine I am forced to drink. With each one I come closer to drowning. I cannot speak. My throat is tight and I do not believe my own hearing.

'Mark —' I begin.

'I know. Her years are very young. There is perhaps twenty five between us. But I have been given a great opportunity, Tristan. A second chance. I have lost my only son and I sit at the head of the feasting table beside a seat that was once reserved for Rufus. Now Iseult sits in his place. I did not realise how much I missed him. There is a chance I could father another child, perhaps even another heir.'

I pull a chair out from the table and sit. Put my head in my hands. Mark continues.

'My life is shortening every day. When, if, I have another son, I would still need you to protect him and rule Kernow until he came of age.'

'You speak as if he is already born.'

The words stick in my throat. Mark is full of hope for a future filled with peace and a wife and children. He longs for what I took from him. For another little Rufus. How can I ask him to give that up? What makes my longing more worthy than his happiness? He is a man more deserving than any I know and yet he has asked for little more than respect from his subjects and his enemies. He has given me everything, and I have given him nothing in return.

'It is not just about children, Tristan, though she is young enough to bear many.'

'I understand. When will you tell her?'

'After we have eaten.'

I embrace Mark briefly and leave.

The sea is dark with no horizon. Clouds shelter the moon. I think of the years I have walked along this shore and wonder how many times Iseult walked her own shores beyond tonight's unseen horizon. The distance is little, and yet she is now in Kernow and the distance is further still. How long since I slept in the damp beside Rufus? How long since I last lay with a woman?

I try to grasp a joyful memory but they are lost to me now. I am resigned, suddenly, to return to Dumnonia and fight again for Geraint. I know my sword. I understand it and it sings for me.

CHAPTER 30

Iseult

Acha brushes my hair, gentle but firm, and I am distant as my thoughts roam their own lands. Lands of Tristan and me and the horse we rode. I think what it would be like to kiss him and I think of his touch and his hand upon my body. He is tender and strong. And I am weak in his presence. Not weak as I was with Morholt, unable to free myself from his rule, but unable to part my mind from thoughts of the man who will be heir to Kernow. A man so different from my Lord Morholt or of any man he led.

'The king's nephew has returned from Ireland,' Acha says. She is leaning close to me, her voice low, as if she is not meant to know, and I wonder how she discovered this news.

'What have my uncles said? Do you know? Are we to return to Ireland?'

'Too many questions,' Acha says.

I take from her answer she knows nothing more.

A fire pours heat into our small room. I grow sleepy and after a while Acha stops brushing and looks through the gowns Tristan's mother has given me. There are shades of red the colour of roses, fabrics of silvery moon, and blue as pale as the sky. I choose gold for the warmth it reflects.

Acha slips the gown over my head and I hope that it is a favourite of Tristan's. That his memories of King Mark's wife wearing the same are not tarnished. I wonder how his wife died and remember the sorrow in his eyes. I cannot remember seeing a man as alone as he.

We arrive in the great hall, Acha and I. People crowd every corner and I think perhaps they have come because of Oswyn's return. I look for Tristan, eager to see his face and assure myself the afternoon I spent with him was not a dream, but I do not find him.

Was it real? I begin to doubt everything that has happened these past hours when a voice behind me says: 'You look beautiful, Iseult.'

The king smiles gently. He looks happier and I think he is glad to see his nephew safely home. He takes my arm and threads a way through the crowd as I struggle to match his stride. Acha follows behind.

At the far end of the hall five tables groan beneath the weight of food and drink. The king leads us to the biggest and he first gestures for me to sit, then Acha beside me. King Mark sits on my other side and still I look for sign of Tristan. Acha scowls at me as though I have been out all night, asleep by the sea. Does she know what overwhelms my thoughts?

King Mark gestures for a man to come and sit beside him. He dutifully does. I think for a moment it is Tristan, but his hair is the wrong colour and his eyes are harder and his walk is stiff and unfriendly.

'Oswyn, this is Iseult of Ireland,' the king says.

I stand for the king's nephew and he takes my hand and presses his lips upon it.

'A fair hand,' he says. His mouth twitches and his eyes sparkle with amusement. Does he jest at my expense?

I say nothing and take my seat. I think the courtesy he has bestowed is one of duty to his uncle and that without the king's presence he may not have acknowledged me at all. I do not like him and I am a little afraid of him. He sits beside King Mark and helps himself to food without a word.

'Please eat, Iseult,' the king says.

I want to ask him what my own uncles have said, but he has turned to his nephew. I hear him ask why Tristan is not present but I do not hear the reply. Has Tristan already asked him if there is a way for me to stay in Kernow?

Beside me, Acha is eating as if she has starved for three weeks. She is enjoying the plentiful food and good wine.

'Five kinds of meat,' she says, her mouth half full.

I smile at the simple pleasure.

I see Tristan then, through the crowd. He looks cold and tired and I try to catch his eye but he does not see me. My heart is skipping and turning and my breath comes quickly. He walks around the edge of the hall towards us, but does not look at me, and then he stoops to speak in his uncle's ear. I see Oswyn's face, cruel and watchful. He is no friend of Tristan, and I see why the king has chosen Tristan as his heir and not this man who would sour wine with his look.

Tristan sits down beside Oswyn, as far from me as possible. I feel my face begin to crease and crumble as I wonder what change there has been since we stood in the courtyard. My forehead burns from his lips and I hold that thought close because I know it was real.

King Mark leans a little closer to me.

'How do you like Kernow?'

Relief. I feel a great surge of it. Tristan has spoken with him of my staying here.

'Very well.' I am keen for him to know of my desire to stay and add: 'I think I should miss the people and the generosity we have been shown if I were to return home.'

Home. I wonder if it is here now. I would like that. To walk the shores that Tristan walks and share the moments I have until now known in solitude.

'I need to speak with you, Iseult. Alone.'

The king stands and gestures for me to follow him. I glance to Tristan, try to catch his eye, but he does not look up from his plate.

We sit down once more in the council chambers that we had sat in when I first came to Tintagel. The king appears awkward as if he does not know how to phrase what he is about to say and I wish that Tristan were here. I do not feel as comfortable alone with King Mark as I did with Tristan.

'As you know,' he says, 'my nephew, Oswyn, has returned from Ireland. He has spoken with your uncles, and they are as eager as I am to reinstate the treaty that was put in place by your father. Their decision is both wise and beneficial to everyone, I am sure you will agree. They will send a force to southern Ireland to see an end to any of Morholt's forces which remain. Your family will therefore be safe.'

Relief fills my heart as I think of my mother. Her position as a woman of the blood will once more be held high and she will likely find a good match amongst my uncles' men. I am happy, I realise, at the prospect of her smiling again. Laughing again. Finding a joy in life that she has not known for such a long time.

'There is more. Your uncles have proposed that we bind our kingdoms with blood. They have suggested a match to secure the peace we so nearly lost when your father died. I will not force this upon you. But I do not think you would be unhappy. They propose that you and I marry and forge more than just a treaty between our peoples. They suggest an alliance.'

I frown. I know I must, for I do not understand the words he has spoken.

'Marry?'

I do not mean to speak aloud but I have.

'It must be a surprise, I know,' the king replies, 'but you have enjoyed your time here? My company, the people, the castle, the sea? You would be as free as you are now, to come and go as you please, to visit your homeland when you choose. What are your thoughts?'

Eyes that betrayed awkwardness now show the smallest amount of impatience. I cannot form an answer. I think of Tristan. Did he not speak with him, did he not plead for me to stay here so that I might be with him, and not the king? What passed between them since this afternoon? I think of the king's bed, and not Tristan's, and the world begins to spin and I try to breathe but cannot.

He stands, touches his cheek as if remembering my touch as I tended his wound.

'I will give you time to think on it,' he says.

There is anger in his voice but mostly longing and I feel sadness for not having pleased him.

'Might I speak with Tristan?'

I do not know what good it would do, and whether I should have asked, but I cannot give answer to this proposal before speaking with him.

The king falters, but composes himself just as quickly.

'I will send him to you.'

As I wait, I wonder what I will say and how this will play out.

CHAPTER 31

Tristan

I do not touch my plate, the food spread upon the table, the goblet filled with wine. My stomach churns and my face burns with shame. I did not look at her, meet her eye. I pretended this afternoon did not happen. That we were not close for a few moments, free of obligation and loyalties.

She is Irish, I tell myself.

An Irish girl that Mark would marry.

What will she say to him? Does she this moment accept the proposal put forth by her uncles? Was this afternoon real?

I cannot think straight. The room has grown dark, the noise unbearable. Tables of men and women speak of rumour and reunion. Servants and slaves rush back and forth. Warriors become merry on drink.

I stand to leave.

'When the kings of Ireland proposed that Mark marry the daughter of Donnchadh, I did not think she would be so beautiful.'

Oswyn leans back in his chair, a cup in his hand, smiling up at me.

I do not speak. I have no wish to exchange words with my cousin.

'I admit I am tempted by the thought of her sitting on my cock too.'

My anger fired, I breathe deeply. Walk away, I tell myself, but I cannot.

'Take a care, Oswyn. Mark would not wish to hear your speak of her in such a way.'

He leans forward in his chair.

'You are smitten with the little Irish girl.' He laughs. 'A woman desired by many. I hear she was betrothed to Morholt before Mark killed him. She has you lusting after her. Now Mark wants to marry her.'

'Mark marries her for the sake of peace,' I say.

Oswyn shrugs, still smiling. 'If that is what you believe. One day you may inherit her as you will the throne of Kernow.'

'Mark's decision,' I spit back.

'Not all of Mark's decisions are wise. If you lose your life in battle as easily as Rufus lost his, my succession is safe.'

'I would kill you now if I did not think Mark had suffered enough.'

'Strong words, cousin.'

I am about to retort once more when Mark appears. He is troubled, his brow creased, his gaze far away. He looks up and catches my eye, must have heard mine and Oswyn's words, but makes no comment. He rests a hand on my shoulder, distracted.

'Iseult would speak with you, Tristan.'

CHAPTER 32

Iseult

Before I can order my thoughts, Tristan appears in the doorway, his expression neutral, unreadable. Surely Mark has told him of my uncles' proposal of marriage?

'Do you know?' I ask.

Tristan takes a step forward, hesitates.

'I owe Mark everything. I cannot ask him to give up his chance of happiness for mine.'

The words are hard, rehearsed. Tristan stands proud and strong and uncaring, as if my proximity might burn him and I feel tears in my eyes. What change has occurred in him that he can be so different?

'You … you said you would speak with the king?'

'He told me that he would ask you to marry him before I had chance.'

'But I wanted to stay here for you, not for him.' My throat is tight. I stand up and take a step toward him, and he takes a step back and looks to the floor.

'Tristan? Is that not what you wanted? Did I misunderstand? Was I so wrong?'

'It cannot be.'

'Your king would understand!' I half scream, half plead.

'No, Iseult. No.' He is shaking his head, as if warding off his own emotion.

Hot tears of frustration roll down my cheeks. I want him to stop this indifference and cruelty, and be the man I rode with this afternoon. More tears come. I long for the jesting and the banter and the affection. I crave the Tristan I know to surface. For nothing to stand between us and for life to be simple.

Tristan breaks. His mask flakes away and beneath he is as distraught as I. He comes to me and brushes away my tears and kisses my forehead.

'Gods know what you have done to me, Iseult.'

He is himself again, the man I know, the one I spent the day with. I am thankful for his return and I am smiling.

'I am indebted to Mark is so many ways. He deserves happiness and there is no other way for me to provide that for him. It is selfish of me to want you for myself.'

I am crying and I am tired. I want him to hold me but I know he will not return my embrace. I look into his grey eyes and find nothing but resignation.

'And if I refuse to marry the king?'

Tristan looks to the floor and sighs.

'You could not marry me, even if I spoke with Mark. It is your uncles' bidding, to gift you to Kernow's king. They would see it as an affront to their wishes if they saw Mark pass their gift to another man. You must have their permission. Without it, we could see war again, so you marry Mark or return to Ireland.'

'I have little choice then,' I say, and tears splash down the dress of the king's late wife. Was his idea to dress me in these clothes, knowing that I would take her place?

'You are beautiful and kind and Mark is the best man I know. I could not wish for a better match for either of you.'

'And what of you, Tristan? What of your future?'

'Mark still attempts to unite the kingdoms of Briton, more so now he is at peace with the Irish once more. Eurig travels to Cunedda's kingdom in the morning. I will go with him.'

My whole body burns with misery and longing and frustration and helplessness. I want him to stay but I do not speak it. His mind is set and I do not wish to make this harder for either of us. I let him leave and brush my tears away and resign myself to my fate.

CHAPTER 31

Tristan

The air is warmer and the birds sing of spring. We ride along an old Roman road north, patched and worn and ill-repaired. Our horses stumble and snort complaint, and after a while I veer off the road and continue on the grassy verge.

Eurig rides beside me. Silent since Tintagel and I have not made the effort to speak. He guesses my mood and my reason for leaving I am sure. I could not stay and see Mark and Iseult wed. The thought of her name turns my stomach, and I breathe deep the fresh, north air and will myself not to think it again. Already I know the decision to leave was the right one. If Eurig knows my feelings, it would not have been long before Mark realised them too.

I saw my mother before I left. She clung to me as though I would not return. She knows too the hurt I feel, the lies I told her, that I travelled with Eurig because I could not bear to stay in Kernow with Rufus gone.

'You are fond of Iseult?'

'As are you.'

I saw her trying to form words that do not admit her suspicions.

'Mark is strong,' she said to me.

'He is,' I replied.

'I do not blame you for what happened to Rufus. And neither

does Mark. You must accept this. I have not seen you happy once since you returned from Dumnonia, except when you were with her.'

She saw more than she acknowledged on the day we rode to the priory. Were my feelings so obvious? Did she see the glow of a summer's day as I spoke with Iseult? Or witness our hands touching?

I feel tired. And bitter. Knowing, as Eurig and I ride north, Mark will be preparing for his marriage. I pray that his happiness is greater than mine would have been.

We cross the border into Ceredigion. Cunedda's kingdom. We have ridden for three days. The skies have turned grey and the air is wetter than in Kernow. Spring seems more distant here. There are no proper roads and the milestones are hard to make out. I hear dogs barking in the distance.

'How far to the coast?' Eurig asks.

'Not far. A couple of miles, perhaps.'

'And from Cunedda's hall?'

'We will be there by nightfall.'

It has been a long time since I was last in Ceredigion. It has not changed. There is still the feel of disrepair and a loss of heart in the people who wander about their business.

The horses trudge on. My cloak is wet. We were in Dumnonia so long, sleeping on the cold mud and sodden grass that I had forgotten the warmth of Tintagel. Now I miss it again.

'What is it we hope to gain from this journey?' I ask. I had not spoken fully with Mark, not expecting to be making this trip.

'Now the Bloodshields are all but defeated, Mark wants to try and unite the kingdoms of Briton and the kingdoms of Ireland.'

I almost laugh. Never have the kingdoms of Briton been united. What chance is there to unite them and those of Ireland?

'That is optimistic,' I say.

'Impossible,' Eurig replies. 'Cunedda has no care for the Irish. But Mark has become infatuated with the Irish girl. He thinks that his marriage to her will make anything possible.'

The mention of Iseult stabs deep in my belly. I find Eurig's observation of Mark's infatuation surprising. Is Mark infatuated? I try to recall his words and remember only a mild interest on his part, driven by the peace he could secure and the son she might carry.

'He can begin again,' I mumble.

'She will not bring him peace. Mark is blinded by her.'

Am I too blinded? Is every man save Eurig taken with her, captivated by her? Mark is an idealist, but he is a rational man.

We reach Caerleon whilst the sun is still high. The journey has been fast, just the two of us. Cunedda's hall is an old Roman fort and I wonder at Roman roads being in such disrepair, filled with holes and crumbling away. In Kernow Mark ensures their maintenance, with our trade and our warriors dependent.

We are received well and fed and our horses tended. I have fought for Cunedda in the past; fought in his place as he sat in his tent and feasted. His men are supportive of him, but his arrogance played a hand in the disintegration of Mark's last attempt at a united Briton.

When Cunedda finally sees fit to grant audience, Eurig and I are shown into his hall. The floor is covered in dirty, stinking rushes, and a dog pisses against a pillar. I breathe through my mouth as we approach Cunedda of the White Hands. He is sat upon a dais, a round, fat belly resting upon his knees, a chicken leg in one hand and greasy beard framing his mouth. On his tunic a white painted hand.

'Tristan of Kernow. It has been many years since you last brought your sword to my halls.'

Too few, I think.

'You look well, Cunedda.'

I see him wince at the informality, but I have no time for this man. His alliance with Kernow would mean little. Mark would be better seeking audience with Demetia or Powys.

'What is it you seek?' he asks.

It is Eurig who replies.

'The Bloodshields are no more. Mark defeated Morholt on our shores a little under a month ago. The northern Irish lords have offered a new treaty with Kernow, and Mark asks you seek the same peace so that we might stand as one against the Saxon.'

Cunedda's face creases and his eyes widen.

'Peace?' he spits. 'Peace? Mark can lie with them if he chooses, but I am not making fucking peace with the Irish. I would rather dine with the Saxon than crawl to the bastards. Fucking Irish. They are never off my fucking shores. Half my fishing boats have to patrol the sea to stop them raiding my people. Half! That's half the fucking people of Ceredigion hungry and nothing to trade. And then I have Powys and Gwent expecting my warriors to defend their lands against the Saxon. My people are starving and they ask this of me! Are the Saxon my concern? Are they? The Saxon do not broach my borders or my shores, they are not my fucking problem. Would Powys build me more ships to defend Ceredigion against the Irish? I think not.'

Not one man in the room is moved by Cunedda's rage. Eurig looks impassive. He knew as I did the answer we should expect.

'The King of Kernow implores you to reconsider,' Eurig says. 'Peace is less costly than war.'

'Paying tribute?' Cunedda barks a laugh. 'I will never pay tribute. Whilst I take breath and my cock is stiff, I will not give them a single coin.'

'The Saxon push closer to your kingdom every year,' Eurig says. 'It will not be long before they reach your borders, and then you will have the Irish on your shores and the Saxon digging a hole in the heart of your lands.'

'They will not get this far. My priority is the Irish. If Mark truly wants peace, I will make it with him. Tell him he can have one of my daughters to bind our kingdoms, but I will not bow to the fucking Irish.'

'Mark is to be married as we speak,' Eurig says, and I note that he does not disclose that he will be wed an Irish girl.

'Then why is he harassing me? Should he not be rutting the bitch? I would piss on Mark's name if I did not owe him for his spears.'

Cunedda speaks of the spearmen Mark sent to aid him and Powys when Luitcoyt attempted to invade two years ago.

'He gave you spears,' Eurig says. 'He did not sell them to you.'

'Maybe not, but he expects me to agree to a truce with the Irish. I would rather piss on them.'

Cunedda will not be turned to Mark's thinking. Eurig does not hold hope of success and does not push as far as Mark would. It would have been better had Mark himself seen that Cunedda could never be turned. Cunedda does not hold grudge with us, and we feast in his stinking hall that night. For all the dirt and muck the hall holds, the food is good and the mead plentiful.

'I have said before and I say again, Tristan ap Mark, I would have you front my defences,' Cunedda says.

'Against the Irish or the Saxon?'

'Both. Either. Pick a man to fight beside and I pick you. Always did.'

I see the irony even if he does not. Little Rufus fought beside me last.

'You know I will not.'

'Still loyal?'

I almost tell him I am heir to Kernow's throne now, but something holds me back.

'Come, Tristan. We have known one another a long time. You used to hate the fucking Irish as much I do.' He leans toward me. Almost loses balance. Mead sloshes on the table and runs through Cunedda's beard. 'Come north and defend my lands. I'll give you one of my daughters and land and spears.'

'Mark's spears,' I remind him.

'Aye, Mark's bloody spears. Your countrymen. They would follow you better than a Ceredigion lord.'

Eurig taps my shoulder. Gives me a withering look.

'I go to bed. We leave at sunrise tomorrow.'

'I will follow soon,' I say.

'Well, what say you?' Cunedda presses. Drink rolls on his breath but I know him serious. 'You can have that one.'

He points across the room and for a heartbeat I see Iseult. Silver hair a halo. Her heart-shaped face.

'Her name is Iseult.'

I am confused now. My mind rolling and exhausted. What trickery is this, to show me a girl who looks the same as the one I met in Kernow? To name her the same?

'Iseult?'

'The second youngest of my four daughters.'

'Her name is Iseult?'

Cunedda studies me through his drunken haze. He is concentrating.

'Iseult of the White Hands.'

I stare at her a while, try to see the difference. She holds herself proud, her eyes a little narrower, but they are the only differences I see.

Cunedda slaps my shoulder.

'Sleep on it.'

CHAPTER 32

Iseult

I stand in the room which will now be mine. Mine and my lord, my king, my husband's. I will not sleep beside Acha again. The room is much larger than the chamber in which Acha and I slept before. Each wall is hung with tapestries denoting the battles the king has fought and many are peaceful scenes of farming and fishing and one is of a child in a cradle. Rufus, I think. The boy to whom I would have been stepmother; the reason I am now married to King Mark and not to Tristan.

The king enters the room and I feel a draft of cold air before he shuts the door behind him. I sense his nervousness, the way he avoids my eye and does not immediately come to me. He is a good and kind and thoughtful man, and I tell myself that I am fortunate to have found a husband who is not at all like my Lord Morholt.

He takes off his tunic and then his shirt. In the light of the fire I see his arms and chest and back are scarred from battle. The lines are pale and old compared to the gash on his cheek, now a closed red line. The times a sword has pierced his flesh I cannot count.

He comes to me. Slow, uneasy. It has been a long time since a woman slept in his chambers I think.

My panic rises as he touches my hair, my neck, the side of my face, his fingers careful and unsure. He closes his eyes as he kisses me on my lips, so unfamiliar a sensation and I am wondering if Tristan would kiss me like this.

I banish Tristan from my head, my mind, my thoughts. I cannot think of him, for if I do I know that I will turn mad. I must think of the king and him alone.

'I have thought of you much,' he murmurs, and begins to unfasten the buttons of my dress and I am awkward and nervous and he is fumbling and nervous too, and for a heartbeat I think I am going to laugh for this grown man is as afraid as I am and it is not his first time.

'Let me,' I say.

He seems relieved as my gown falls to the floor and I blush at my own nakedness.

He leads me to the bed and pulls back the blankets and I lie down. He smells of freshly tilled earth and honey. I am less nervous now, of his gaze upon my body and what is to come. Tristan's face fleets in my thoughts over and over and each time I push it away.

The king kisses me again and I do not know how, or do not want to respond. I do my best, and he seems pleased with that, and he is suddenly naked now too and moving between my legs and I am afraid and wishing that Tristan was here instead, for I know that with him I would be nervous, but I would also be excited.

There is difficulty, at first. I lie on my back and he fumbles and I am wincing although the pain is not so bad. I want to please him, but for the first time since being in Kernow I want to go home to Ireland.

I begin to cry.

The king does not notice at first, his eyes closed and his face full of concentration. When he has finished and pulls away and opens his eyes, he sees my tears and his expression is one of horror.

'What have I done? Are you hurt?'

I wipe my tears and the king moves away and pulls the

blankets over me as if this will cure whatever is wrong.

'You have not done anything,' I say. 'Forgive me.'

His expression softens and he lies down beside me, his back to the fire, arm across my stomach.

'You are not hurt?'

'I do not think so.'

I wonder if I would have enjoyed it, as he seems to have done, with his warm glow and sense of satisfaction.

He does not speak again and after a while falls asleep.

I watch him, the rise and fall of his chest, his dark beard twitching, listening to his inward and outward breath and the crackling fire. I was always going to be married for my blood and my position and here I am and I stay awake for hours and hours, until the fire has died and I hear the morning cry of the birds beyond the window.

I must fall asleep, and when I wake in the morning the king is gazing at me.

'Are you happy, Iseult?'

It is a question I have dreaded. To be asked to quantify the feeling and to know that this man's happiness is hinged on mine. I think of my Lord Morholt and it makes the lie a little easier.

'I am, my King.'

He smiles. 'You can call me Mark, you know.' He kisses me. 'The title is nothing, and besides, you are my queen now.' He kisses me again. I realise suddenly that his kisses are an advance but I am unsure how to respond.

'Mark.' It feels odd, the name without the title.

His mouth is eager, more so than the previous night. It is as though he is determined in his endeavour, that perhaps he knows I do not desire him in the way I desire Tristan, or he feels the same, and we must work harder at our intimacy in order to make it real.

Mark looks at me as he moves inside of me, and I wonder as

his eyes search mine, whether he is looking for an answer to an unspoken question. Does he look for the last queen of Kernow in my eyes? Does he seek my affection or just another child?

When it is over, he lies on top of me a moment, still and heavy. He strokes my hair from my face and kisses me once more.

My guilt has begun; I do not share the same feelings I think Mark has for me. And I wonder what will become of us.

CHAPTER 33

Tristan

The following morning Cunedda assures me that his offer of marriage to his daughter is a genuine one. He owes Mark, and would bind his kingdom to Kernow above all others. He asks me to stay in Caerleon longer, but Eurig is to return home and I have no desire to journey alone.

We ride and I think of Iseult of the White Hands. Silver hair and smallest frame. She is my Iseult's twin, too fair and too pure to live in Cunedda's stinking hall. Could I save this Iseult, this other woman, from a worse match made by her father on another drunken night? Could I give this Iseult the life I would have given mine?

I clear the thoughts from my mind. Look at the road. Look at Eurig. He watches me.

'You did not tell Cunedda you are now Mark's heir?' he says.

'Should I?'

'No. But he offers you positions that you could never accept as the future king of Kernow.'

My suspicion is roused. Does he speak of Iseult of the White Hands, and the marriage match, or fronting a Ceredigion defence against the Irish?

'Cunedda speaks of what he wants. He is a plain man.'

'He speaks too freely,' says Eurig.

The sun blisters cold morning air. The roads are drier and

firm beneath my horse's hooves. Something has changed; the lie of the land, the rise of the hills, the babbling spring becks. I think of Iseult, and the husband she now has.

Our brief connection has ended. Their marriage now consummated. Emptiness takes hold.

I am tempted to turn back. To say to Eurig that I … That I what? That I do not feel I can return home? That my desire for Mark's new wife is so intense I cannot master my feelings? Or do I lie and feign I am too ill to travel? What curse is this that I cannot face Mark and Iseult united? Should I not feel happy for Mark and indifferent to Iseult? I wish I did. I wish that she had never travelled the sea from Ireland. Never smiled at me.

I resign myself to facing them and feeling no emotion. I will embrace them both as family and live my own life. My thoughts darken. When I am king, when Mark is gone, would she be with me then?

I curse the gods. What foolish thoughts and selfish notion. In which kingdom is it right to wish your king and uncle, the man who has given you everything, dead. For that I hate myself.

As we near Kernow I realise every thought, every moment of the journey, I have thought of Iseult. The flowers I have seen I would pick for her. Early lambs bleat and I am reminded of her tenderness. My horse whinnies and I watch her soothe him. I see a stream and think of her kindness to my mother, and I witness dogs fight and think of her tending Mark's wounds after fighting Morholt.

Will it stop?

Do I want it to end?

I crave to spend time with her. Even now, knowing she is Mark's, I am eager to see her again. I will be the man I know I can be. I will call her friend.

CHAPTER 34

Iseult

I sit on the shingle of the shore and look out toward Ireland. Blue skies and white clouds trail across the sky and the wind is calm as it pulls back my hair. Acha walks the beach behind me but I sit here and think of my mother. I might ask Mark if I can visit her soon.

Acha longs for Ireland, but she does not say. She walks the shore more than I do now and I see her looking, as if waiting for a ship that would take us home. I am a queen now, but Acha is still a servant and she does not find a place amongst the Britons easily. There is hatred amongst many, and the kingdoms here hate one another, and the religions hate one another too. I cannot confess to understanding the politics of which Mark speaks or his toleration of every god.

I hear someone shout and turn to see a figure on the horizon. Acha is some distance away by the sea, so I know it is not her. It must be Mark, I think, come to spend time with me on these shores; to take away the time I saved for myself. I do not wish to share this space, this shoreline. I am not inclined to sit and talk, but let my mind run free and travel the waves and back again. This is my space, my home, the shingle of my shores.

The figure is closer and I see that it is not Mark. The man is leaner, taller, and my heart is racing.

I am on my feet and half walking, half running, toward him and as his features become clear I see he is smiling.

'Tristan, I did not know you had returned.'

I should not, but before I know it I have embraced him and he holds me for a heartbeat before pulling away and he looks at me as if trying to remember something.

'I thought you might be here.'

'I miss Ireland.'

'Only Ireland?' he grins.

'I missed you a little too.'

And there it is, we are talking as if he has never been to Caerleon and I have not married Mark. I had been afraid it would stop, and we would not be the same two people, that the connection we had found would end. But it is there, as it was before, and I am relieved there is no awkwardness between us.

'How are you finding life as the Queen of Kernow?'

I am not sure to which part his question refers. I think of my intimacy with Mark and blush. Even saying Mark's name before Tristan seems wrong.

'I am becoming accustomed to it,' I say, guarded. 'The Kernish are friendly enough. Did you find success in Caerleon? Mark says you hoped to secure an alliance.'

'Is that all Mark said?' He is grinning at me.

'He said that he was hopeful you would succeed, as the king was in his debt.'

'Cunedda is, yes. But he is also a very stubborn man. He did not agree to what Mark wanted. And there is little more to say.'

We walk for a while. Tristan does not speak of Caerleon further. He is keeping something from me, I can tell. What agreement did Mark desire? I think to ask him at the next opportunity.

I shield my eyes from the sun's glare as we make the ascent back to the castle. I remember the first time I walked this slope, Tristan and Acha beside me, slipping and sliding in the mud, fearful of our fate. Tristan began to consume my thoughts then,

I think. As he helped Acha. It was a month ago, yet I feel I have known him all my life, so familiar are we.

Tristan takes my elbow as we climb a difficult part of the path. And as I take my skirts and struggle with the shoes I have been given by Isabel, he takes my hand too.

Sword-born callouses brush gently on the soft skin of my palm. His fingers are strong and take my weight as we climb together.

We reach the top and he lets go my hand. We walk silently along the path back to the castle. The waves and the gulls and the sea breeze a pleasant music to our pace. And when we reach the castle we pause a moment, and with great effort I say:

'I am glad to see you home. Shall we walk again tomorrow?'

'I would like that.'

And with those parting words we go our separate ways.

CHAPTER 35

Tristan

I wait on the rampart. Look inland toward the priory. I cannot see it from here, but my mother has gone again, this time with Mark, and I see the rustle of their horses through the woods as they leave.

Mark spoke to me again of his confining my mother there with the sisterhood. He says she desires it, but I know that she does not. She wants only a place to grieve for little Rufus.

Below me, the courtyard lies empty. I am early, but still I glance every now and then, eager to see Iseult and to walk with her on our shores. We have walked each day for three weeks. I know that each time we venture onto the beach and our feet crunch on the sand and stone, our time together becomes harder because I want her more. I am too comfortable in her company, becoming more dependent. Yet I do not decline her invitation. I can no more resist her than I can bring my cousin back.

'Tristan!'

Her voice surprises me. She is early too. The sun has not yet moved to its highest point. Nor did I see her approach. I hurry down the steps from the rampart and she smiles in greeting, and the day becomes a little warmer.

Summer months approach. The ground finally firm and the grass growing faster than the sheep can eat.

'It is a glorious day,' Iseult says.

'Not that the weather stopped you venturing to the shore yesterday.'

'It is only water.'

Through the gates we walk and out onto the open road. Mark has asked me to go back to Dumnonia, this time with Eurig, and I am unsure how to tell Iseult I will be away a while. I have grown too fond of her company and I suspect, or hope, she has become fond of mine also. Perhaps it is good that we are forced to a little time apart, that the ache I feel to touch and hold her will be less.

'Did Mark not want you to accompany him and my mother to the priory?' I ask.

'I told him that I do not believe in the Christian god. He seemed happy enough with that.'

Would she have gone with Mark, had she not preferred to spend the time walking with me? Is that what she meant? I think it, but I am not sure.

'I am worried my mother goes there too often now.'

'Mark presses her to stay with the sisterhood.'

It is as I suspected. Mark still wishes her to send her to the priory. Out of sight and mind. To live out her days with lonely women and pious priests.

'I heard.'

'Do you think she should?' Iseult asks.

'It is not my wish, no. Mark does not believe in their god, yet he gives much lenience to them. I think he would put faith in any priest or god that might relieve him of the grief he bears for Rufus. My mother being here, in the castle, reminds him too much. She wears her sorrow too openly for him.'

'He does grieve for Rufus, in his own way, in private,' she says.

I think of his confiding in her and immediate thought turns to the intimacies they share. Not a pleasant thought. I try to turn my mind from it, without success. I think of Iseult of the White hands. Could I stroll on her shores, as I do now, exchanging words, sharing company? At ease with one another? I still want my Iseult standing beside me, even now she is wed to Mark.

We walk back, seaweed tangled beneath our feet. Iseult's hair glowing bright. I have never walked these shores so much. Grassy verges, rocks, paths; they are as familiar as the scars I earned adventuring as a child.

Almost at the castle and I steel myself to tell Iseult that Mark is sending me to the Saxon frontier, to Dumnonia, once more. Then Mark and my mother ride toward us. Mark bellows greeting and waves. My mother looks sicker still, as if plagued by a physical illness as well as grief.

Mark dismounts. A servant runs to take his horse's reins.

'You have walked the shores again, Iseult?' he asks.

'It is a beautiful day.'

He kisses her. I look away, awkward, unable to control the sickness which rises like bile in my throat. How many times must I witness their intimacy before I cease feeling emotion?

'I would speak with you, Tristan.'

I follow Mark up the ramparts leaving Iseult and my mother in the courtyard. I dread what Mark is about to say, wondering first if he suspects my attachment and longing for Iseult. Is it obvious? Does he know I have walked with her each day? Or does he wish to speak of my mother being sent to live in the priory?

He pauses at the top of the rampart steps, only just out of earshot of my mother and Iseult, and the men patrolling the walls. I look down at the sea lapping the shore and the paths I trod with Iseult. What was once my home where I returned to escape the aftermath of battle and the torrent of emotion is fast becoming a place filled only with longing.

'You will not be travelling to Dumnonia with Eurig,' Mark says flatly.

'Why not?'

'Because I will go with Oswyn instead. We have our treaty with the Irish so it is not essential I remain here. I think it better that my presence is known in Dumnonia, and Geraint could well be influenced more if I am to take command of the Kernish contingent of the defences. It is no reflection of your ability or anything else, only that it has been too long since I ventured beyond my own lands, and it is necessary for a king to be seen abroad sometimes. You will come to understand this.'

I wonder at his leaving Iseult so soon after their marriage. Is their bed a happy one? If I were him I would turn away every petitioner to spend my time with her. They are all I ever think of. Iseult, Mark. Mark and Iseult. Gods, the constant plaguing of my mind aches.

'What of me?'

'You will stay here in my place. You will be King of Kernow one day. It is time for you to take command of the people and be known as a man who can run his country as well as lead warrior bands.'

He takes Oswyn with him to save me the trouble he would cause. A shrewd decision. Then I think of staying here with Iseult instead and the torment I would know. The past weeks I had foreseen travelling to Dumnonia. Thought the sickness I felt seeing Mark and Iseult together eased, because I would not have to spend time near them. I craved that space, to breathe, to focus on the enemy and free my mind. Now I would not have that. Or am I secretly pleased at the uninterrupted company? It is hard to know.

'There is something I did not tell you when I returned from Caerleon,' I say. And now that I have said it, I know I must go on. 'Cunedda did not wholly refuse your offer of a treaty. He would bind himself to Kernow and to Briton, but not to the Irish.'

'He is already at peace with the Britons. He is too indebted and owes too much coin, especially to me.'

'He would have the same bind that you now have with the Irish.'

'Go on.'

'He proposes that I marry one of his daughters.'

I am not sure what I hope to achieve. Whether I want Mark to agree, to disagree, suggest I leave and strip me of the title he has bestowed. Instead his expression relaxes, as if relieved.

'My boy, I have waited a long time to hear that. This new marriage alliance could see more stability to Briton than you know. This is great news. I would see you as happy as I am. For all that I have heard of Cunedda, I believe his daughters are beautiful.'

'There is one. Her name is Iseult.'

Mark pauses, a little surprised. Confused, perhaps.

'Iseult of the White Hands?'

'A coincidence, I know.'

'This is the one you would marry?'

I nod. I watch the waves rolling in, one after another. The sea which brought my Iseult here.

'You will live in the castle?' he asks.

'You misunderstand, Mark. We would not live here. I would go to Ceredigion and front Cunedda's defences. It would give us greater control over their movements, perhaps one day result in a greater peace.'

Mark's face appears broken. He turns his back on me and when he speaks his voice is angry and hard.

'Tristan, you cannot leave Kernow and live in Ceredigion and still be heir to the Kernish throne. You cannot simply return when I am dead and assume the role. There is work to be done here, with our people, to ensure the transition of power is smooth. You know that Oswyn would not allow you to set foot back on Kernish soil as a man, never mind a king, when I am gone.'

'I know this.'

He turns back to me. 'Then why? An alliance with Cunedda is no more valuable than your rule here. You must see that.'

'I cannot be the person you want me to be.' The words are

true enough, but my omissions are heavy with guilt.

'Of course you can. I lost Rufus, now you, is that it? If I can bear his absence then so can you, Tristan.'

'That is not true, not the reason I leave. I will be in a neighbouring kingdom. You said yourself; you may yet bear another son who will become heir.'

'And you would have been his guardian.'

'I will go, Mark. This is Cunedda's offer and I have chosen to accept. '

He nods his head. Tired and defeated.

CHAPTER 36

Iseult

I see Mark and Tristan high on the ramparts. I know Mark speaks with Tristan of leaving for Dumnonia, and that Tristan will stay here, with me. I was unsure at first, Mark gone and Tristan and I sharing our days alone. Then I thought of the past few weeks and the walks we have had and the time we have shared and felt relieved that it would continue if Tristan stayed and Mark went in his place.

Isabel speaks to me, but I do not hear. I am watching, waiting, wondering what is said. When they have finished Mark does not return to where I wait, and instead walks along the far side of the rampart. I think to follow him, but Tristan appears.

'Might I speak with you, Iseult?'

'Of course.'

Isabel embraces Tristan.

'It is for the best, that you stay here,' she says. 'I could not bear to lose you too.' Then she leaves.

We walk back the way we came in silence. Tristan looks away from me, distant and thoughtful. His loose shirt billows slightly in the breeze.

'Mark has already told me he will go to Dumnonia,' I say.

Tristan sighs. A long, heavy, mournful sound.

'I will not be staying here, Iseult. I am going back to Ceredigion to fight for King Cunedda.'

'But why?' my voice is edged with hysteria, but I cannot hold it back. Fear rides within me. Not anticipation or excitement, longing or desire. Just fear of the words I am willing not to follow.

'Because I cannot stay here with you.'

'What do you mean?' I ask, my voice uneven. 'What is it you want?'

'Nothing. I want nothing from, nor would I ever ask anything of you.' He pauses. 'I know I must be hurting you, because I am hurting every day. I never meant for this. I knew before we rode to the priory together my feelings. I want to spend every fragment of every day with you, walking the beach, looking out to sea, but you must know that it is hard to be close and yet never close enough. I live on the outskirts of your life, afraid of seeing you with Mark. Please, Iseult, you must understand it is a shadow of a life for me. We cannot pretend any longer that there is nothing between us.'

'Why Ceredigion?'

'I am to marry.'

There is silence for a long time as I inhale his words. Become sick on them. Feel the jolt as they hit the pit of my stomach and I cannot breathe. I look into his face and sense he is waiting for me to reply, but I have nothing to say. Nothing that will make my own pain dissipate, nor stop my heart from crying.

'My apologies,' he says.

His words sound strange, rehearsed. Is this the way he feels, or is it just pretence? What happened to the walks we shared and the laughter we had? How has it suddenly disappeared?

'There is no need for an apology,' I say.

'There is. There is so much to apologise for. I am sorry that I did not speak up to Mark and tell him how I felt. But I could not. After Mark forgave me Rufus' death … He needs you more than I do, Iseult.'

I want to cry, but I hurt too much for tears to come. I want him to make things better. To take back what he has said. How could he, I think. Making me want him, turning his back because of his guilt, forcing me to feel a marriage to Mark was my only choice. I am angry with him, with myself, with Mark and with everything in this world. I am saved from Morholt but still I am not free.

'Every day is hard,' Tristan continues, the creases of his face echoing his words. 'I am trying to make it easier for us both. I am trying not to spend the rest of my life a bitter man, taunted by your presence.'

'Taunted?' the word catches in my throat. 'But my bitterness will never cease, will it?'

'No, it will not. Not if you keep it close.'

'Have I a choice?' I say, and recoil at my own, venomous tone.

Tristan grips my hand and squeezes.

'I cannot spend my whole life wishing I was with you. The gods know I want things to be different, but we both know that cannot be. They are laughing at us, you know. We must amuse them greatly.' He laughs a little. 'Now I am trying to make something of my life. I am trying to start afresh, from nothing, and learn how to be content with someone other than you.'

They are the hardest words I have ever had to hear. Tears are running freely down my face. I am ashamed of them, embarrassed at my feelings, knowing he will care for another in the way he cares for me.

'I will never stop wanting you, Iseult. To me you will always be something extraordinary. Something special. You have a piece of me that can never be taken back. You will own it for the rest of your life and beyond, if you want it.'

My throat is tight and I cannot speak. I look at the ground, wanting it to swallow me whole and suffocate the flames.

Finally, I manage a little nod.

He wraps me in his arms and holds me tight. Tighter. Then lets go.

I grip his hand again and he kisses it.

'And when you return, you will be married,' I say, forcing a light tone into a constricted voice.

Tristan glances to the ground.

'I will not return, Iseult. I forfeit the succession to the Kernish throne.'

His grey eyes meet mine. I am unable to speak. The bottom of my world drops away and there is nothing to catch my fall.

'And will you fight my uncles for King Cunedda?' I ask, more spiteful than I ever thought I could be.

Tristan closes his eyes. 'I do not know, Iseult. Perhaps. The Saxon, the Irish. Does it matter?

'Mark would never let you leave his side,' I say. Then realise the futility; the selfishness. 'But ... you have already spoken with Mark?' I continue, angry with him, with myself, with it all.

'Yes.'

I nod. As if it all makes sense. Feeling like I already knew this. That I was waiting for it to be spoken.

'When do you leave?' I ask, not really wanting the answer.

'A week from now.'

'Will I ever see you again?'

'I do not know what will happen. I am sorry, but I cannot promise what I do not yet know.'

I pull my hand from his, the world turning and turning and I cannot see. I cannot breathe. I want it to stop. I want to plead with him not to go, but what right do I have to ask him to stay? I can give him nothing. I can never be his. But the hurt is unbearable and I do not know how to make it all go away.

'Forgive me,' I say, and turn to leave.

My heart beats faster than a running hare. So fast it is almost a blur. My legs are weak and I am unsure I can walk back to the keep, but somehow I manage. Up the grassy slope. Away from the man I care for above all else. Away from the man I cannot imagine leaving.

'Iseult!'

He calls my name and the wind plucks it from the air and carries it toward me. Each syllable a distinct imprint of his voice in my mind.

I do not turn back.

My vision is obscured and I am sobbing.

CHAPTER 37

Tristan

Iseult and I barely speak. She does not seek me out, and neither do I approach her. Our heated words and the tears I caused compound my guilt. I have been selfish. Forced Iseult into a marriage with Mark because I could not bear to see his grief and feel the guilt I should have felt. Instead I wound Iseult. What made me believe her pain would be less than mine? Did I realise her marrying Mark would feel so utterly despairing?

Now I intend to leave.

It is best, I tell myself: to leave and let them start their lives afresh.

Mark comes to my rooms as I pack, sits on the edge of my bed. The lines of his brow are deeper as he watches me.

'Is there any point to my persuading you to stay?'

'I am grateful for everything you have done for me. But my mind is made up. This is my path.'

Mark exhales, heavy and tired.

'All right. You will report to me often, let me know the situation in Cunedda's kingdom?'

'Of course.'

He stands, our conversation at an end. He embraces me.

Awkward. A shirt still in my hand.

'Take care, Tristan.'

Once I have finished packing I seek Iseult. There are things I must say, though I am not sure what. To wish her well, to say something of a goodbye? Whatever is spoken, I would rather it was out of Mark's hearing.

I find her with my mother, working on a tapestry in the tower. Another passage of time Mark will forever enshrine to the walls of his rooms. I thought his documentation of life instead of living it had passed with Iseult's presence. It seems it has not.

I watch a moment, her nimble fingers stitching the face of a young man. For a heartbeat I think it Rufus, then I realise it is me.

'A fair likeness,' I say.

Iseult startles.

My mother says: 'This tapestry is for me to remember you by, Tristan. I have already stitched Rufus.'

Her voice near breaks, so fragile are her words. I wish I were a boy again, sat cross-legged at her feet, listening to her tales. Those times are gone. I steady myself with the thought of my own children and the stories I will tell. Of what? A cousin lost, a woman I could not have, and a kingdom I should have ruled?

'I must have a word with the kitchen,' my mother says.

She leaves, her eyes telling me she extends the same courtesy Iseult once gave her.

I sit down on my mother's stool. I think to take Iseult's hands in mine.

Should not. Do not.

'Iseult …'

'There is nothing to say, Tristan. Live your life. I am happy for you.'

Her words are gentle, sad. She stares at the thread in her lap, playing it between her fingers.

'This is why I must go. It is too much. We both know that. So many reasons why we cannot be together … Please, never think that I do not care for you.'

'I know,' she replies, her voice forlorn.

She must know as I do how unbearable it would become if I stayed. Better to forget until another time. Better to pretend it never was.

I reach out and brush her fingers with mine, and she grips my hand. This is the closest we will ever be, a light touch of fingers; all I will have to remember her. She has never been mine, even when I rode with her, held her, kissed her forehead and walked the shores each day. But I am hers. There is a piece of my heart she took for her own the day she came to Kernow. Once hers, she moulded it so that it would never fit back.

'Come to me,' I say, 'when you are your own woman and may go where you wish. There will always be a home for you with me if you want it.'

'You will be married, Tristan.' Her face is wet with tears and the light in her eyes dies as I sit there. I pull her toward me and brush the tears away and feel such sorrow.

'I am sorrier than you can know. For everything. Come to me, when you can. You will always have a place and I will always think of you, I promise.' I feel her nod against my chest. 'I will watch the sea every day for your boat. You do not have to come yourself. Raise a white flag and I will come for you. Raise a black flag and I will know that we are not to be.'

She pulls away from me.

'I will come. I promise.'

When my lips touch hers there is no restraint.

Then I leave to start afresh. To wait for her.

PART TWO

20 Years Later

CHAPTER 38

Tristan

The summer sun warms my face and neck. Flies buzz. A nearby stream plays a tune, trickling, brushing, splashing over stones. A serene sound, of a day I should be working to a solitary rhythm and pace on my lands. How I crave the peace of my own company. Instead I stand with my back to a line of Ceredigion warriors waiting for the Saxon.

Behind the Ceredigion are men of Gwent. To our right and left stand Powys and Luitcoyt spears. Beside them men of Demetia and Elmet and Buellt. Almost all the tribes of northern Briton. United. Determined that this summer the Saxon will be pushed back and the heart of our lands reclaimed.

We stand high up, knowing they approach. Waiting for the sound of drums and the hum of marching warriors. I am not nervous. I do not feel the same fear the younger warriors know. My years have been spent living on one frontier or another. This will be my last battle, I think. A man's body can only take so many blows on the front line, and mine has taken many. I feel the deep cuts to my arms and legs in the winter. The cold biting. I am stiff in the morning and exhausted in the evening. And these Saxon are becoming accustomed to our terrain, pushing harder, familiar with our lands, calling them *home*.

I breathe deep the scent of grass, almost smell the sea. We are many miles inland. I miss the coast, the estate I bid Cunedda grant me there, the breeze, the salt, the horizon; they have become my escape.

A haze forms in the distance. The Saxon will travel this road through Luitcoyt, I am sure. Beside me, Eurig grows restless. He shuffles from one foot to the other. Flexing his sword. Adjusting his shield.

'They will come, Eurig.'

'They had better. I was sent for news of your talks with the Irish, not to stand in a shield wall again.'

'You relish it; otherwise you would not be here.'

'I am here because I did not wish to wait in Cunedda's stinking hall for your return.'

His relaxed face and slight smile tell me he is enjoying the frontier. I know he feels alive when he is in the north, with his sword and his shield and a mind free to face the enemy.

'Do not worry, Eurig, I will send you home soon enough. Then you can fall back into retirement.'

His smile fades.

'There are things you should know of home, Tristan.'

'Stop!'

Eurig knows better than to speak of the life I left behind, to utter the names of the people, or deliver news of them.

'Do not speak, Eurig. I will not hear it.'

He falls silent. Just as I think he is about to ignore my word and speak of Kernow, scouts appear on the road, riding hard.

'They are on the road,' the first to reach me says, breathless, as he reins in his horse.

I nod and dismiss him.

I hear them now, in the distance. The gathering warriors fall quiet. The ground feels unsteady. Cunedda would spit on my uniting the kingdoms of Briton if he were here. But he is not, bound to his halls by sickness and old age with no son of his own. He would curse more if he knew of my peace talks with the Irish when he believes I ride the waves warding them off.

Mark crosses my mind. I know I do this for him and all that I owe him. I am tired, but he must be more so. He craved a united Briton and Ireland, the creation of a force powerful and strong enough to repel the invaders who try to take our lands. Here we are. I look about me and see tides of men swarming the hill and wonder what Mark would think if he could see this: so many kingdoms together as one. That is why I asked Eurig to come. To see what I have achieved in the north, to take the news back to Kernow and know that we all are brothers in common cause.

Murmurs ripple through the ranks. Word reaches me. The keener eyes now see the enemy. Flags wave overhead. Voices shout to stand firm, not to move, not to run raging at the enemy and lose our advantage.

Barking.

The Saxon bring dogs. How I hate their mutts.

They lead the way, yelping, snapping, pulling. Behind them the Saxon spread out along the road. They scream and shout and curse in their language I have never understood.

'See to the dogs,' Eurig says.

'You giving orders now, old man?'

Eurig grunts. I do as he says, wave an arm overhead and a heartbeat later shards of death whistle through the bright sky. The dogs yelp and cry as the arrows strike home. A handful of the enemy fall too.

'Come and die!' One of our men shouts. Another takes down his pants and waves his cock at them.

'Your northerners know how to torment the Saxon,' Eurig says, laughing.

'Oh, they do,' I reply. 'Just wait.'

Sorcerers push to the fore of the enemy lines. Their robes held above their knees, feet hobbling as if dancing on hot coals. Screeching, crying, wailing.

My heart beats faster.

I am not afraid of the sorcerers. Their magic and curses do not trouble me. I am anxious for this battle to begin, and if I do not want to lose the higher ground, the enemy must come to us.

At last, as the sun peaks and begins to dips, the Saxon find courage and charge.

Their war-howls sound distant. Their movement slow. They reach the hidden trenches we dug two days ago, halfway up the slope, and the first lines of Saxon fall. Men behind stumble, and the men behind them are disorientated and trip over their brothers.

We charge.

I run almost too fast for my legs. Gaining speed. Holding tight my sword, a shield strapped to my arm. The Saxon are scrambling over their own, the trenches packed with their men. They bare their teeth and so do I. A snarling growl, lips curled, spittle flying and then we crash together.

The gods roar as a tide of iron strikes iron. Two thousand Saxon are crushed by the momentum of five thousand Britons charging down the slopes of their homeland.

Hot breath hits my face. My own, gasping and hard. We are man against man now. One sword against another. Battle-din raging. Screaming and shouting. Curses. Rage. A mixture of noise that must be heard in every kingdom.

I take an axe-blow to my shield, push it away, bring up my sword and rip through the first man. Another strike, low down. I jump, punch down with the edge of my shield and up with my sword tip. Red rivers pour from the man's mouth, down my arm. And again, I slice. Blood, warm and wet, sprays across my face and chest.

'Tristan, damn it, watch your back!' Eurig shouts.

I turn. Sunlight bouncing off a blade blinds. I am deep in the Saxon line, the enemy flanking me, closing in behind.

I scream my war-cry, a sound loud enough to shake the heavens and bring thunder on this hot day. I punch forward with my shield. And again. Feel it crunching into a Saxon face. I push the man back into the one behind and bring my sword in low. He has no furs to protect him. He growls back as if I have not cut him in two. Then the rage vanishes from his mad eyes and he drops.

I cut down two more with ease. The aches I know fade for a moment.

The enemy is thinning.

Eurig kneels on a man and parts him from this life. Stands. He drips with Saxon blood, sinew, scraps of flesh.

'I am too old for this.' His breathing is laboured but he recovers quickly.

'I need to see what is happening.'

We scramble back up the slope. The first twenty paces slicked dark green, slippery and wet. When we are high enough I look across at the swathes of men, my men, the united men of Briton, and the Saxon buckling beneath the press of their spirit.

I knew the Saxon were outnumbered, yet seeing the armies spread before me I understand suddenly Mark's hopes for peace and cooperation between our countrymen. He knew. He understood this would be the only way to save Briton. Peace with the Irish meant we could concentrate our force on a common enemy.

My sword hangs limp in my bloodied hand. Sweat stings my eyes, but it is stained red. Will this be our last stand? Will we now see a peace of sorts? I think of Mark sitting in his council chambers and the news Eurig will bring him as I watch the remaining Saxon retreat back along the Roman road. See our men slaughter the rest, cutting, slicing, ripping iron through flesh and bone. What will Mark think? Will he be proud?

This was his dream. Not this blood, but the hope blood brings.

Is it my dream now?

As much as I try to convince myself, I know it is not.

CHAPTER 39

Iseult

I sit in the darkness of the king's chamber. It is the last day Mark will inhabit this world. Lying in our bed his eyes roll beneath their lids, his lips ride up and show his gums and his face is waxen and yellow. Though he is older than me, with the Otherworld pulling him away he looks older still. Flesh drapes the bones of his face, fluttering with every breath.

I think of Mark reaching for his sister and his son in the Otherworld. Isabel died in the Priory two months after Tristan left for Caerleon. In twenty years I have written to him only once, to tell him of his mother's death. I told him she died of fever, but that was not true. She died of a broken heart and I could not bear to think of Tristan's guilt.

Acha fumbles wood on the fire, creating a noise that would wake my husband were he sleeping. Instead he groans as though the end of the world is upon us.

'Pass me his sword,' I say.

Oswyn puts a hand on my shoulder. His touch is as tender as the farmers aiding the lambing in February, and yet I know how many innocent lives that hand has taken; how much blood has run down his blade in a bid to prove himself.

'The sword will pass to me when he is gone, Iseult.'

'He has not gone yet,' I say.

I lay the sword on Mark's chest and place his hands upon

it. All warriors should die with a sword in their hand. And my good and caring king needs his sword if he is to claim his rightful place in the feasting hall of the gods.

My reflection looks tattered in the bright iron. I am old now — almost thirty-six — and because of my infertile womb Oswyn will inherit. The gods punish me. Tristan has never left my thoughts and the gods know this and they would see me barren and unable to provide for Mark. And yet Mark never banished me, never left my bed nor questioned my sadness. Never once have I walked with him on the shore, for that is the place I save to think of Tristan, but he has been kind to me and I have grown fonder of him each passing year.

I kiss Mark's lips and my tears spill onto his cheek.

'Iseult?' My name is a hoarse rumble from deep inside him.

'Save breath to greet friends in the feasting hall.'

I take his hand in mine and look into his face. I see the scar gifted by Morholt's blade, and think of the day I pressed cloth to the wound, more grateful than he could ever know.

'Thank you,' I whisper, 'for everything.'

The blade rises on Mark's chest seven times and then rises no more.

I already know what I will do next. I have known for a long time.

CHAPTER 40

Tristan

I part with Eurig on the outskirts of Ceredigion. Head onward for the coast and home. Cunedda can discover the outcome of the battle from another, as I have no desire to visit his halls and face his disgust at my alliance with neighbouring kingdoms.

My lands lie in a valley on the west coast, facing the Irish. I feel the sea air as I approach. For the first time in two months I can rest.

I reach the edge of my estate and my horse urges onward, the sloping fields, low walls and narrow road familiar to us both. My house sits as idyllic as ever, accompanied by a scattering of outbuildings and tenant dwellings further afield. Eanfrid, my estate manager, in the yard with our horses. He waves.

'Good to see you, friend,' I say.

'And you, Tristan.'

I enter the house, sit in a chair at the kitchen table. I am dirty and tired, scratched and bruised. I have a broken rib, a cut on my leg and two more on my arm. All I wish to do it sit.

Iseult of the White Hands comes into the kitchen. She carries a pail of water.

'You are home?'

'I am.'

She ladles a little water into a bowl, sits down beside me and bathes the scratches on my body. There is little tenderness, just a methodical need to clean the wounds.

I reach forward for bread and cheese, a cup of ale.

'I worried you would not return to us.'

'We outnumbered them,' I say in answer.

She purses her lips, disapproving. It has been a long time since her lips curved and her scowl relaxed.

'You should take more care,' she says. She wrings the cloth in the bowl, leaves the table.

'Next time, I will. I am too old for this.'

Her scowl deepens. I do not ask what it wrong. I drink the ale and chew on the bread as if she does not stand watching me.

'Word has it you have sought peace with the Irish,' she says.

'I have.'

'Against my father's wishes.'

'I have done many things against his wishes.' I look at her, sigh, wonder if she will ever understand. 'Iseult, think of what it could mean. No more war, no more raids. Ceredigion could be wealthy with revenue from fishing and farming, instead of having to find coin for spears and struggling through the winter. Uniting with Powys and Gwent and the other kingdoms has already seen victory over the Saxon and the reclaim of lands that we have not trodden in years.'

'My father is king of Ceredigion, Tristan, not you.'

'Cunedda is on his deathbed.'

Iseult throws the cloth into the bowl of water.

'Do not speak of him as if he is already dead!'

'He will be soon,' I reply. 'That is why you still sit at this table and sleep beneath this roof. Because you know that my men are the strongest force in Ceredigion and the whole of northern Briton. They might be under your father's rule, but they are my men, loyal only to me. And without an heir, the strongest warlord will take his place. You not only stay because of it. You wanted it.'

I chop wood in the forest. Sweat breaking. The marks of battle breaking open, weeping as I work, regretting my words to Iseult of the White Hands as I have done so many times. I came to Ceredigion to fight for her father, yet I have fought to better his kingdom and benefit the whole of Briton. Neither understand. Should I have expected them to?

Cutting wood reminds me of my son. Eight years old with an axe twice his size, stood with me in this very spot. Who could know that winter would be the harshest we had known, that a weak chest would claim him? I wonder often if she hates me more for the death of our son or because she knows I do not long to be with her. Perhaps both …

'My Lord! Tristan!'

Gods be damned, but I cannot get a moment's peace. I turn to see Eanfrid running up the embankment toward me. He is so old and unfit he needs to pause and catch his breath every few feet.

I drop my axe and bellow back: 'What is it, friend?'

When he finally reaches me, sweating and gasping, he cannot speak.

'You need more exercise, old man,' I say, smiling, trying to forget my thoughts.

'My Lord, the king is dead.'

The words tumble from his toothless mouth and my hand slips from his shoulder.

Thoughts churn slowly in my mind. The death of kings brings change, and no one can tell whether it be good or bad until the warlords have finished jostling and the order of power settles.

'Then we must pay tribute to Cunedda. I must gather those loyal to me and make my presence in his halls known.' I pick up my shirt and wipe my brow.

Eanfrid is shaking his head.

'King Cunedda still lives. The King of Kernow is dead. I speak of Mark.'

Hearing the name forbidden in my house for near twenty

years teases a flame somewhere inside me.

I pick up my axe. 'Keep a lookout on the cliffs. Tell them to watch for a single boat. There should be a flag raised. I want to know the colour of that flag.'

Eanfrid leaves and I am alone with my thoughts. My heart races faster than a rabbit. Mark is dead. I wonder if Eurig knew him unwell as we stood facing the Saxon together. How long has it been since I was last in Kernow? Too long, I think. I sold my services to Cunedda and have spent many days since wishing I had not. Does Iseult of Ireland, of Kernow, still think of me? Is she well? I burned all letters she and Mark sent. I could not bear news of home. But I remember our promise, clear as if I had just spoken it.

Everything has changed. Everything is different.

Will she come, I wonder? Will she stay?

CHAPTER 41

Iseult

The morning I intend to leave Kernow, Oswyn comes to me.

I stand by my coffer, folding clothes and preparing for my journey. I pick up the tapestry depicting Tristan's face that Isabel and I had made. It is a poor likeness, but it reminds me of him. I put it on the fire and watch it catch. I do not need it now. I look at my hands. They are lined and wrinkled and dry and worn. I have changed. Childless, and still my belly hangs soft.

'Which part of Kernow proves so undesirable that you flee, Iseult?'

I look into Oswyn's face and think how much he looks like his cousin. But Tristan was noble. He protected us and fought for Mark and when he chose to leave he went without complaint, leaving Oswyn the throne that should have been his.

'There is no place for me here now.'

'Then I shall make one for you,' he says, moving toward me.

He is the same age as me, but I have spent many years sleeping beside his uncle. His hand on my breast and his greedy mouth pressing on my lips surprises me. Nothing then reminds me of Tristan.

I put my hands between us to ease him away. Our mouths break apart.

'There is no need to make a place for me. I do not require one.'

The strike which follows throws me to the floor amongst gowns and linen. Oswyn hits me again. Fear grips me as he presses his knees between my legs and then I hear my own shocked gasp.

I learned a long time ago to feel nothing, to take each moment as it came and know that each one would bring me closer to my destination. I think of this now. Another obstacle on my path to Tristan. I will be gone from this place soon enough. And still the shame and anger wells in my eyes.

Acha appears in the doorway. Her mouth is open and she looks about to scream, but I give a little shake of my head. It is too late; the painful thrusting has stopped.

He kisses me, as a lover would after such exertion. And I think how I hate him more than I hated Morholt.

Acha moves out of my vision and I look at Oswyn and feel scorn as he diminishes inside me. A tear rolls down my cheek as his fluids trickle down my thigh.

'Even after all this time,' he spits, 'you would you go to him, Iseult of Kernow?'

'To who, Oswyn?'

He sneers at me as he has done so many times before.

'Mark told me there was a connection between you and Tristan. How could he think my weak cousin would ever be a king? When he told me what he had done, that he had named Tristan heir, and of your obvious affection for one another, I knew I could not let you be together.'

'It was Rufus' throne, never yours.'

'Who do you think spoke in Mark's ear and persuaded him to send the weakling to the frontier? Who do you think told him that the boy could never be a king if he did not see battle? And who told Mark that your uncles desired you to marry the king of Kernow? You could have married any lord. You could have married Tristan.' He smirks, pleased with himself.

The revelation does not shock, I do not feel sick on his words. I am free now and I will leave here and I will never look upon him again.

CHAPTER 42

Tristan

I sit on the cliff top waiting for the ship with the white or the black flag to appear on the horizon. None comes. I have been here five days. I have neither slept nor eaten. I look away, hoping that when I look back to sea she will be there, that I will see her white flag. I do not worry of the frontier. Of the peace I craved before. I wanted that for Mark.

Mark, the man who thought of me as a son.

I am ashamed that I could not stay at his side, to serve him, show him loyalty. But I have done my best from afar. I have begun to bring together the tribes of Briton.

'You are still here, husband?'

Iseult of the White Hands stands behind me, and I know she regards me with detestation in her eyes. For every moment I do not work the land, or serve her father, or fight the Irish, she looks at me in that way.

'Yes, wife, I am here.'

'I hear rumour we are expecting a visitor?'

'Eanfrid told you?'

She clicks her tongue with impatience. I take a deep breath.

'We are expecting a girl ... a woman ... She is wife of King Mark. Her name is Iseult.'

I do not look at my wife. I do not want to see her face as I breathe the name *Iseult*. To hear the difference in the way I say the name of my Iseult compared to hers. To know that I married her for her name and her face to ease my own aching, as she married me for my sword.

There is a pause that stretches two lifetimes before she snaps, 'King Mark is dead.'

'So I am told.'

'Why does his wife come here?'

If only she would snap at someone else. Then I think of poor Eanfrid, and know that if she is not cursing at me, she is bleating in his ear.

'Because she has no home now that Mark is dead. And I made a promise to her, a long time ago, that I would give her a home if she ever needed one.'

'She cannot stay here.'

'If that is your wish,' I reply, knowing that I would leave this place if my Iseult still wanted to be with me. Leave the fighting, the treaties and home I made. I would leave it all to spend my remaining days with her.

'When will she come?'

'I do not know. She will come on a ship with a white flag,' and my heart trips as I speak, 'or send a ship with a black flag to say she is not.'

My wife leaves, and I look out to sea and think of the irony. Not only does my wife have the same name as my queen, but she looks so much like her too: both with hair of silver blond and eyes so blue to be almost violet. And despite this, I could not feel more differently about the two. In which life did I think I could marry another Iseult and be as happy as I was walking the shore with Iseult of Ireland?

Perhaps my two Iseults look nothing alike now.

CHAPTER 43

Iseult

I leave as soon as Oswyn returns to our frontier.

There are more bruises on me than I realised as I struggle to the boat. I planned this journey so many years ago that it feels as if I have made it before and every excited beat of my heart is followed by a beat that sends a trembling through me. The boat master smiles as I place coin on his palm to have him raise a white flag.

I look back as we drift away from the coast. The wind makes my eyes water and tears stream from their corners and into my hair. I see the shore that I have walked along every day for more than twenty years. I can still remember the weeks I spent there with Tristan. The day that Mark fought Morholt and the years of gratitude I spent in his company. I remember Tristan, soaked through, walking up the muddy bank back to the keep and embracing his mother. What has happened between then and now? The Saxon still push forward, the tribes of Briton are yet to be united, my countrymen still raid the northern coast, and my feelings are as they have always been.

Nothing has changed.

Or has it? Eurig spoke of tribes united. Was it true?

This journey will only take a few days and yet for me it has taken years.

Will Tristan recognise me?

I worry for the moment we meet again and cannot help but wonder about the disappointment I will be, or whether he has thought of me at all. They were just words, I tell myself. A promise of two young, foolish people; a promise that meant more to me than to him?

And what of his wife? He married the King of Caerleon's daughter, that I know. Did they have children? I worry that he is happy and that he will turn me away.

I do not sleep at night. I envisage him coming to meet me on the coast as I step from the small boat onto the shingle of his home. I think of his embrace, a memory so faded that I can barely remember what it was like; barely remember his scent and his voice and his face.

CHAPTER 43

Tristan

Eanfrid finds me in the yard. I am seeing to the horses and he lingers. When I look up, his expression is awkward and he can barely hold my eye.

'Say what you came to say.'

'I have seen the ship.'

Words fail me. I do not want to know the answer to the question burning my throat.

'The flag is black,' he says, before I have chance to enquire.

She does not come. The world falls away and there is nothing beneath my feet. I stand there, an empty man, twenty years of hope and longing crushed by a breath of news.

'All right, Eanfrid. Leave me.'

He hurries back into the house and I am alone with my horse. She is old, but she is of the same temperament as her mother, with whom I rode to the priory so many years ago.

'It is all right.' I stroke her flank and she whinnies. 'Shhh.'

I had been captivated once more by the girl with playful humour. I was captured by a wish that would never be realised. For a long time all I had thought on was her caring expression, her smile, her hand in mine. It is strange; to know a ship sent by the Iseult I had cared for all those years ago and for all the years since crested our coast with answer for me. With promise.

I stumble across the yard and out of the gate. I think to go to the shore, but I do not want to see the black flag upon the horizon. Instead I walk across the fields and to the forest. Foliage casts shadow on the mossy ground and tree roots trip me. The dagger I pull from my boot is a gift from Iseult of the White Hands. It slips easily from its sheath, used every day. I look at the blade and see the reflection of an old man with greying hair and a weathered face, whose life has gone by in a flurry of hope and regret.

She remembered. She thought to send word either way.

CHAPTER 44

Iseult

Birds sing the song of the waves as I step out of the boat. Water laps at my ankles and soaks my dress. The place is strangely quiet as the boat is pushed back into the water, leaving me alone on the shore. There is no one to greet me, even though I sent word ahead that Mark sat in the feasting hall of kings. I tremble. *Come on, lass*, I say to myself, and realise it is Tristan's voice in my head.

I walk up the slope to the grassy ground and from there I see his estate in the distance, deep in a valley. Are all shores so similar, I wonder; heavy salt on your lips and crunching shingle?

Almost forty years the daughter of a king or married to one, and now I walk like a peasant, alone and muddy with a bag on my shoulder. A traveller. I do not mind, I am filled with hope and excitement and longing.

I reach the estate and I know my Tristan has made good account for himself. He has worked these lands and fought for King Cunedda, and been rewarded with this place of beauty in a land of poor.

A man called Eanfrid introduces himself. He has an honest face, but nervous, and is rounded and red and exerted.

'Tristan ap Mark?' I say, 'He is expecting me.'

Eanfrid looks at me curiously. 'You are Iseult of Kernow?'

'I am,' I say, pleased that Tristan has told him of me. Relieved that he has sent this man to welcome me.

'You have no place here.'

The words are those of a woman standing some distance away. She approaches and I see her face is the same shape as mine and her eyes the same colour but they are cold.

'I seek Tristan ap Mark. Can you tell him Iseult has come?'

'Tristan of Caerleon is dead.'

The world turns to ash, fire gone, light dead. I am angry that he has done this to us. That he cared for his uncle so much he would not hurt him, and instead hurt me.

'Tristan?' I manage to say. 'Tristan, nephew of King Mark of Kernow?'

Her face is as hard as the flint that pierces my heart and drags through my innards.

'The very one.'

I am shaking, my legs weak and heart racing and hurting and tight. I sit beside my Tristan, his body lain on a table in his house. Light from the window shines on his face and I almost believe he is sleeping beneath the thin veil of linen. His face is the same as the last time I saw him, lines and creases of age faded in death. I wonder does he wave from the ferryboat, bidding me join him.

'He left Kernow because of you.'

Iseult of the White Hands stands in the doorway. She does not enter the room. She is afraid, I think, of the man lying upon this table, of his death that cannot be undone.

'He did.' It is my first admission of what passed between us, and now I make it to his widow.

'He would have left me had you come.'

I stroke Tristan's face, my hands whiter than the linen.

'How could you know …?'

'I knew. He was always distant and forlorn. His heart did not belong in Ceredigion; it was claimed long before he met me.'

My eyes weigh heavy and I imagine myself lying beside

Tristan as he sleeps.

'I claimed only a piece of his heart.' I say. 'The rest belonged to Mark.'

I sit in silence. After a long while I say: 'How did he die?'

'He took his own life.' Her voice is bitter.

'How?'

'He told me you would send a ship with a white flag to tell him that you would come, or a black flag to say you were not. He waited on the shore day and night for you. Two days ago I could take it no longer. I had Eanfrid tell him he had sighted a ship bearing a black flag.'

My rage rushes and threatens to drown me. Tears stream down my cheeks as they must hers.

'I am sorry,' she says, 'I did not foresee this.'

The soft pad of her footsteps tells me she has gone. I think to follow, but I do not think my legs would carry me. I stay beside Tristan for hours, recounting the days, despair crashing into me, not knowing what to do or where to turn.

'I came,' I whisper. 'You said there would be a home with you if I wanted it.'

I watch his still form, willing him to move, to answer, for this not to be. How close I came to seeing him again. How near. He was my hope, the person for whom I lived each day.

'I am sorry, for everything.'

I kiss him one last time and leave.

I walk in the woods amidst the hazel and the honeysuckle and sense my Tristan all about. He has walked these paths. This is the closest I have been to him in twenty years. Sun peeps through the leaves of the trees and strokes my cheeks and neck with a warmth that feels like his hands holding my face.

I have no food upon my person or provision on my back. I am at the end of my journey and I will rest. My eyes close and I see them: Tristan and Mark, my mother and Isabel, little Rufus, the boy I never met, sat in the feasting hall of the gods, laughing and merry. The ferryman stands in his boat, a welcome lantern drawing me onward. I open my palm and find coins and he takes them from me. He offers me his hand and guides me into the boat. I take a last glimpse of the lands I have known and know that I do not want my place in Kernow, and I have none in Caerleon. I will take one last voyage and find my place with Tristan.

THANK YOU FOR READING A TRISKELE BOOK.

Enjoyed *Tristan and Iseult*? Here's what you can do next.

If you loved the book and would like to help other readers find Triskele Books, please write a short review on the website where you bought the book. Your help in spreading the word is much appreciated and reviews make a huge difference to helping new readers find good books.

More novels from Triskele Books coming soon. You can sign up to be notified of the next release and other news here: **www.triskelebooks.co.uk**

If you are a writer and would like more information on writing and publishing, visit **www.triskelebooks.blogspot.com** and **www.wordswithjam.co.uk**, which are packed with author and industry professional interviews, links to articles on writing, reading, libraries, the publishing industry and indie-publishing.

Connect with us:
Email admin@triskelebooks.co.uk
Twitter @triskelebooks
Facebook www.facebook.com/triskelebooks

Also from Triskele Books

COMPLICIT

'On the beach stood the adverse array (of Britons), a serried mass of arms and men, with women flitting between the ranks. In the style of Furies, in robes of deathly black and with dishevelled hair, they brandished their torches; while a circle of Druids, lifting their hands to heaven and showering imprecations ...'

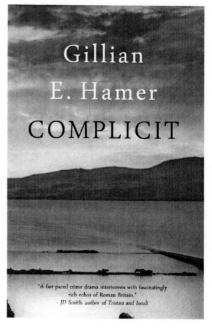

Gillian E. Hamer

COMPLICIT

"A fast paced crime drama interwoven with fascinatingly rich echos of Roman Britain."
- JD Smith, author of Tristan and Iseult

When Roman historian, Cornelius Tacitus, recorded the invasion of the small island of *Mona Insulis* off the North Wales coast in 60AD – the beginnings of a propaganda war against the Druidic religion began.

Two thousand years later, that war is still being fought.

For two millennia, descendants of a small sect of Anglesey Druids have protected their blood lineage and mysterious secrets from the world. Until members of this secret society are murdered one by one.

Detective Sergeants Gareth Parry and Chris Coleman, along with new girl, DC Megan Jones, must stop this killer at all costs. What they discover will shock the whole police team and leave consequences which have an impact like no crime in the history of the force.

Set along the dramatic Menai Straits, *Complicit* is a story of greed, loss and obsession.

Also from Triskele Books

TREAD SOFTLY

*"You don't attract trouble.
You go looking for it."*

Disheartened by her recent performance, Beatrice Stubbs takes a sabbatical from the Metropolitan Police for a gourmet tour of Northern Spain. In Vitoria, she encounters a distant acquaintance. Beautiful, bloody-minded journalist Ana Herrero is onto a story.

Beatrice, scenting adventure, offers her expertise. The two women are sucked into a mystery of missing persons, violent threats, mutilated bodies and industrial-scale fraud. They are out of their depth. With no official authority and unsure who to trust, they find themselves up to their necks in corruption, blackmail and Rioja.

Beatrice calls for the cavalry. The boys are back, and this time, it's a matter of taste. But when her instincts prove fallible, Beatrice discovers that justice is matter of interpretation.

Also from Triskele Books

GIFT OF THE RAVEN

The people of the Haida Gwaii tell the legend of the raven – the trickster who brings the gift of light into the world.

Canada. 1971.

Terry always believed his father would return one day and rescue him from his dark and violent childhood. That's what Indian warriors were supposed to do. But he's thirteen now and doesn't believe in anything much.

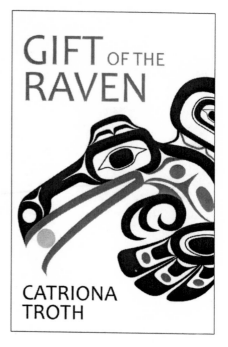

Yet his father is alive.

Someone has tracked him down. And Terry is about to come face to face with the truth about his own past and about the real nature of the gift of the raven.

CPSIA information can be obtained
at www.ICGtesting.com
Printed in the USA
LVOW08s0125081216
516330LV00002B/191/P